A TIME FOR LOVE

A TIME FOR LOVE

BY

AMANDA BROWNING

MILLS & BOON LIMITED
ETON HOUSE   18–24 PARADISE ROAD
RICHMOND   SURREY   TW9 1SR

First published in Great Britain 1992
by Mills & Boon Limited

© Amanda Browning 1992

Australian copyright 1992
Philippine copyright 1992
Large Print edition 1992

ISBN 0 263 13088 6

Set in Times Roman 16 on 16¼ pt.
16-9207-60023 C

Printed and bound in Great Britain by
William Clowes, Beccles, Suffolk.

CHAPTER ONE

THE sound that drew Claudia from her semi-doze was the peal of childish laughter. She became aware of the sun on her back and the sand beneath her toes—and more squeals. No! The groaned denial filled her brain. Nobody knew of this beach. That was why she came here when she needed to charge her emotional and physical batteries.

She had just spent a gruelling six months criss-crossing the Atlantic, attending endless meetings with lawyers, visiting the various foundations she had concerns in. She felt totally drained, in no way able to cope with emotional turmoil—especially not to have it thrust upon her in this fashion. Sitting up, she shaded her eyes.

The child was playing in the shallows not fifty yards away. A girl of no more than seven or eight. Claudia watched her in awful fascination, then closed her eyes in pain. Her mind pictured another child of the same age, whose features were hazy and undefined because she had no photo of her, nor ever would have.

It was too much. Scrambling to her feet, she dragged on baggy white shorts and green silk top over her bikini, thrusting her feet into her sandals. She didn't care how abrupt her departure might look as she gathered together her belongings. All she knew was that she could no longer stay there. Dumping everything into the Ferrari, she climbed behind the wheel, started the engine and shot away with a squeal of rubber.

Tyler Monroe's ultramarine eyes watched impassively as the distant shape of the distinctive red sports car began the descent of the zigzagging road. Sunlight glinted off the gleaming metal and the rock-strewn hillside as the driver took the tight turns at a speed which bordered on the insane.

The breeze off the sea many feet below lifted the dark locks of his jet-black hair and brought to him the rhythmic sound of the ocean, the sighing of the Lombardy poplars— and the now audible throaty roar of the car engine coming ever nearer.

The red streak had reached the bottom by now and proceeded to cover the long curve of the bay at close to a hundred m.p.h. Even that barely brought a flicker of emotion to his cleanly sculptured features. It was a proud face, with a rugged handsomeness. The jaw was strong, forceful, but the mouth was surprisingly sensual. There was the merest hint of a cynical curve to it as he turned to keep that dart of red in his vision.

As the Ferrari took the last curve before passing from view he had the fleeting glimpse of deep chestnut hair flying in the wind before it was gone, leaving only the sound of the engine echoing in his ears. Seconds later silence reigned, and he turned, long legs encased in faded jeans braced as he bent forward. The rolled-up sleeves of his silk shirt revealed strong tanned forearms, the open neck allowed a glimpse of the mat of dark, silky hairs of his chest. Hands spread against the cement of the stone wall that divided the terrace from the cliff, he waited.

There was a definite smile on his lips now, but it was grim and it failed quite noticeably to reach his eyes as he stared out to sea.

Claudia brought her car to a gravel-scrunching halt before the villa and stared darkly at the Alfa Romeo already parked there. Her hands tightened momentarily on the steering-wheel. She had hoped the house would be empty of guests for once, but it seemed she was wrong. Then, with a swift change of mood, so common to her these days, she decided that company might be a good thing after all. Her flight from the beach had been pointless. The thing she had been escaping from had been like the devil on her shoulder. She couldn't go fast enough or far enough—it was always there, her constant companion.

Her work couldn't take up all her time, however hard she tried to make it. There were always periods of frantic activity, closely followed by weeks of idleness. It tired her out but it also lowered her defences, as that incident proved only too clearly. So perhaps company was what she needed. Anything that would take her mind off the past. And if that failed she could always invite friends over. Although the villa belonged to her Aunt Lucia, Claudia knew she wouldn't mind. Lucia adored parties, and for Claudia herself they could be blessedly numbing in times of stress.

Gathering up her beach-bag, she climbed out, slamming the door closed then crossing to enter the cool shade of the hall. White-walled and green-roofed, the sprawling villa was a haven in the hot days of high Italian summer. The stepped terraces made their way gracefully down the sloping cliff to the shimmering blue of the pool. Beyond that, many feet below, lay the sparkling waters of the Ligurian Sea.

Claudia had returned here six years ago like a wounded animal, and in time had found a measure of peace that saved her sanity. But her life had altered. Perhaps it would be more true to say that the life had gone out of her. What existed now was a shell of her former self, that went down the days in an endless search for the unattainable. She worked hard and played hard, and yet there were always moments like today that reminded her she was just a beautiful empty shell.

That statement held no vanity. For she was beautiful. The gilt-framed mirror she stopped before confirmed that without giving her satisfaction. Claudia groped in her bag for her brush and attempted to bring order to the lush waves of chestnut hair that fell to her shoulders. The wild drive had brought colour to the golden tone of her skin—a natural colour due to the northern fairness of her father and the Latin lushness of her mother.

Apart from that, there was very little of her father in her, save for her height and slimness. She had the free hip-swinging walk so vividly seen in the young Sophia Loren. Her waist was slender too, and her bust full and firm. In her early teens this burgeoning womanhood had been a trial to her, but these days she simply accepted the voluptuousness of her figure with barely a glance. Who knew better

than she did that high cheekbones, large
brown eyes and full lips didn't bring happiness? It was fleeting at most—a chimera,
that, once gone, left only barren emptiness
behind.

Only, of course, it wasn't empty. There was
still guilt. That gnawing, destructive guilt
which still slowly eroded her inch by inch, day
by day. A constant wearing away that she
knew would eventually leave her broken and
useless. If there had been any mercy in the
world it would have been over six years ago,
but she had survived. She knew *that* was her
punishment—a long torment was the price she
had to pay.

The soft slap-slap of footsteps brought
Claudia back from those dark memories, and,
squaring her shoulders, she turned to face
Seraphina, her aunt's housekeeper. Dressed
in black, with a snowy-white apron, the
plump woman stood a respectful distance
away, her hands crossed below her ample
bosom, a faint frown darkening her cheerful
face.

'You're back early, *signorina*,' she
observed.

Claudia turned to drop her brush in her
bag, masking a wry twist of her lips. 'The
beach grew too crowded, so I decided to come
home. I see my aunt has visitors.'

'The *signora* has gone to Genoa. The gentleman arrived, asking for you, an hour ago. I told him you were out and I couldn't say when you would return, but he insisted on waiting.'

Claudia frowned a little, looking past Seraphina as if she could probe the thick walls and see who this visitor was. Clearly he was a stranger, or the housekeeper would have said. 'Did he say what he wanted, or who he was?'

Seraphina shook her head. 'Only that he wanted to see you, *signorina*. He is silent, this Englishman.'

Englishman. That brought a swift jolt of surprise to her nerves, but she dismissed it briskly. It meant nothing. She met men of all nationalities. She had probably met this one at a party somewhere and he had looked her up on the strength of it. That was due mostly to the reputation she had acquired when she'd first come to Italy. Her subsequent lifestyle had never erased that beginning. Certain elements of society had long memories. Still, she had become adept at putting people right.

'Where is he?'

'By the pool, *signorina*. Will you change first?'

Claudia glanced down at her shorts that left a long expanse of tanned legs in view down to her sandalled feet, and the baggy silk top. 'I'm decent enough. We'll have coffee on the patio, please, Seraphina.'

Clucking, the housekeeper went away, shaking her head. Claudia smiled at her retreating back. After years of working for the Assanti family, Seraphina still hadn't lost her old-fashioned ideas of propriety. Not that either Claudia or her aunt would dream of laughing at the older woman, for they loved and respected her too much. She was more like one of the family than just a faithful and trusted servant.

Passing through the house, Claudia stepped out on to the patio and shielded her eyes from the sunlight with her hand as she sought for her visitor. She spotted him almost immediately, a solitary figure with his back to her as he stood looking out to sea.

Something in the way he stood made her lower her hand slowly to her side. Her heart kicked. There was something vaguely familiar about the set of his shoulders and the proud lift of his head. A sensation that grew in certainty as she made her way down the terraces towards him. Without her seeing his face, that tautly muscled frame, broad shoulders and slim hips, spoke of a man of considerable strength, both physically and mentally. Here was a man who knew exactly who and what he was without needing to prove it. He exuded a powerful attraction that she felt even at that distance.

She had known only one man who had that potent combination. Only one man possessed that male virility to such a degree that it shimmered about him like an aura. And, knowing that, Claudia slowed her steps.

Tyler.

As if her silent utterance of his name reached him with all the power of a clarion call, he straightened, turning slowly to face her, his eyes spearing her where she stood before taking a leisurely perusal of her frozen figure.

Frozen with shock she might have been, but Claudia felt his eyes in every part of her. It was like sunstroke, and she shivered in the heat as a powerful wave of emotion swept through her, clenching her muscles, tingling along her nerves, leaving her heart racing. Once she had loved him with every atom of her being. He had given her the greatest joy— and the harshest pain when he went from her life. She had tried so hard to banish him from heart and mind. But now she realised that nothing was forgotten. Despite everything, she responded just as she had that very first time, with all the passion of her nature. She had never been indifferent, nor ever could be.

She knew it, but life had taught her many painful lessons. The most important to remember now was that this man could not forget, nor ever forgive the past. Whatever had brought him here was not love or anything like it. So, schooling her features into a smooth mask, although she knew she could do nothing about her pallid cheeks, she moved again to close the distance between them. Hungrily her eyes ate him up. He was all she remembered, even down to the dark blue eyes that had once blazed with a passion to equal her own. But those days were long gone; only a chilly remoteness remained, turning him into a stranger. She halted some feet away.

'Hello, Tyler,' The greeting sounded appallingly husky to her ears, as if her voice were rusty from disuse.

'Claudia.' No glimmer of warmth there, just the terse use of her name.

Nothing had changed. Not that she had expected anything different. In Tyler's world there was only black and white. She was beyond the pale, and destined to remain there. Long dark lashes fluttered down to hide her reaction. 'What are you doing here, Tyler?'

Leaning back against the coping, Tyler crossed his arms. 'Admiring the view,' he drawled sardonically, gaze dropping to her shapely legs.

Claudia stifled a gasp as colour stormed back into her cheeks. There was an insolence in both words and look that she had never received from him before, and she stiffened automatically with the shock of it. A reaction that caused him amusement and had her chin lifting in self-defence. 'You've seen my legs before; they're no mystery to you.'

He inclined his head with a mocking smile. 'Perhaps not, but you were always damn good to look at, Claudia.'

Her eyes widened. This was a different tactic. He had learnt new ways to hurt her in the years since they had last met. To be looked at with love was one thing, this quite another. Instinctively her arms crossed in a purely feminine gesture of defence. 'If I'm supposed to be flattered, I'm not. Just tell me why you're here, Tyler, then go. I don't have time for these senseless little games of yours,' she retorted with all the hardness she could muster.

'Why? What's on the schedule tonight? A wild party or a midnight dip? How fortunate that Italy abounds in fountains. It will take you a lifetime to sample them all. Quite a career move,' he mused contemptuously.

Claudia winced at his reference to the fountain incident. It had happened soon after her return to Italy. Her wildness then had bordered on the manic. So many crazy things done out of desperation. In a reckless moment, after an all-night party, she had cooled off in one of Rome's larger fountains—fully clothed, but the water moulding her dress to her had made an eye-catching sight, and unfortunately there had been a photographer present to make full use of it. The next day her exploit had made the front page of the newspapers, and the ever-rampant paparazzi had religiously recorded every event since.

Her outrageousness had mellowed, for time did heal some wounds, but her reputation was made. One she wasn't proud of, but had become used to shrugging off for pride's sake. Which was why she now plastered on a brittle smile. 'You'll have to wait for the papers tomorrow, like everyone else.'

'Thanks, but I'll pass. These days you're becoming rather repetitive, darling. In fact, you're in danger of becoming a bore. What's gone wrong? Is the fast lane beginning to pall? Is that why you push your car to the limit—searching for thrills? I watched your arrival; you drive as if there were no tomorrow.'

Unwittingly he had scored a hit. The smile faded and her eyes slid away from the challenge in his. She moved to the wall and leant on it, looking down at the undulating sea.

'There's always tomorrow. "To-morrow, and to-morrow, and to-morrow,"' she quoted tonelessly. An endless succession of them. 'If you're worried that I'll crash, or drive over the cliff, don't. Fate has other plans for me,' she added, feeling his burning gaze on her profile.

'It's a dangerous conceit to believe you live a charmed life,' Tyler observed coldly.

That was very nearly funny. 'A charmed life? I suppose it would look like that to you.' The truth was harsher. The sins she had to pay for would take a lifetime. There was to be no sudden ending of it tomorrow.

'You survived one crash. It's all we're ever allowed.'

Claudia paled as he probed the old wound that would never heal. Yet, as ever, she hid the despair behind a cool mask of disdain. 'Why have you come here, Tyler?' she demanded, for the third time.

All pretence of mild manners left him now as he faced her with a look that registered all his contempt. 'Right this minute I'm damned if I know. I took great pleasure in forgetting your very existence. If it weren't for Natalie that's the way it would have stayed.'

Claudia's heart stopped beating, and she went cold. The face she turned on him was white—stricken. 'Who?' The word was a whisper of disbelief as the name tore through her, ravaging every sensibility.

The violence in his face was terrifying. 'Damn you, was it so easy to forget? Natalie. Try to remember her, Claudia. Remember Natalie—your daughter!' His contempt lambasted her.

Claudia swayed as pain assailed her from all sides. She could feel herself shattering into a million irretrievable pieces. She didn't care that her face revealed a soul in torment. 'You bastard! You rotten b——' The word broke on a tortured moan, and she turned and fled back up the terraces, running until every breath was a pain and her heart threatened to burst. Tears turned the path ahead into a trembling, distorted snake, and she stumbled constantly, only to scramble to her feet and carry on, wanting, needing only to escape.

But there was to be none. Her own ragged, sobbing breaths had drowned out the sound of pursuit. She only knew Tyler had followed her when two strong hands caught her arms, biting hard to haul her back just as she reached the patio. Weakly she flailed arms and legs to fight herself free, but it was useless. She never stood a chance against Tyler's formidable strength. Finally she was forced to stand still, chest heaving with her efforts, eyes shut tight on scalding tears.

From behind her, Tyler's voice was a taunt. 'Still running, Claudia?'

'I hate you!' The words sobbed through her trembling lips.

'The feeling is entirely mutual, darling. However, I came to talk to you about Natalie, and talk about her we damned well will!' he declared forcefully as she flinched.

What was he trying to do to her, destroy her utterly?'Natalie's dead!' she cried out, voice breaking on the terrible admission.

'Doubtless it's been convenient for you to think she was,' Tyler shot back contemptuously.

Her heart knocked violently in her chest as, with terrible slowness, the import of his words broke through the wall of her guilt. She half turned, eyes filled with confusion, hardly daring to think of believing. 'W-what do you mean?'

'What do you think I mean?' he taunted, freeing her to turn and face him.

'Damn you, stop playing with me! How can you be so cruel? You never used to be. Natalie's dead. I should know. I killed her!'

Tyler froze, eyes narrowing on the tears that fell unashamedly from her eyes. He frowned. 'Natalie's no more dead than you or me.'

The blunt statement took her breath and drained her blood. Sweat broke out all over her and flies started to buzz madly in her head. With an inarticulate cry Claudia crumpled into a boneless heap as everything went black.

The world infiltrated her unconscious mind with the crack of a whip, and drew Claudia reluctantly back to reality. She moaned as she fought her way out of the blackness and into the light, for a moment not able to remember where she was and why. She felt the hand that was repeating the measured slap on her cheeks and moaned again. Instantly the hand left her, slipping beneath her shoulders to lift her. A glass pressed against her lips and a familiar voice urged her to drink. With no will left to fight, she obeyed and almost gagged on the brandy that slipped down her throat, but the fiery warmth had the desired effect.

Opening her eyes, she focused them blearily on the back of Tyler's head as he turned to put the empty glass down on the coffee-table. Still muzzy, she studied the lush growth of hair that fell over the collar of his shirt. As if a switch had been flicked on she felt her pulse begin to race at memories of running her fingers through it. Without volition she raised a hand to run it into the thickness of his hair. She had no will to stop herself; it was as if a powerful magnet was compelling her to follow its invisible pull.

'Tyler.' Her husky, warm tone gave away her delight at touching him, the feel of his arm beneath her triggering off spirals of pleasure that surged life back into her nervous system. The brandy had warmed her inside, and the caressing motion of her hand set up a delicious languor all through her body. This was Tyler, and she loved him. She wanted him as she had no other man, nor ever would.

'What the hell do you think you're doing?' The harsh words broke the spell she had woven about herself.

Painful colour washed in and out of her cheeks as Tyler rose abruptly and strode away from her. Full memory returned as she struggled to sit up, finding she was in the small salon, on the sofa, where Tyler must have carried her after she fainted. Fainted because he had given her a shock she wasn't prepared for. For seconds she had been lost in the past, forgetting harsher reality. Forgetting...

Her eyes flew to his. 'Natalie? Natalie's alive?' She hardly dared voice the question, lest he now denied it.

Tyler's lips thinned as he watched her from where he stood by the fireplace. 'She's alive,' he confirmed.

The tears came then, flooding down her cheeks as she was totally unable to control them. Claudia raised her hands to her face as something inside her which had been dead for six endless years came alive again. Natalie, her beautiful Natalie, was alive. She could scarcely believe it. Yet she knew Tyler wouldn't lie, for even his hatred was honest.

At that she caught her breath, the tears ebbing away. Realisation dawned, leaving her reeling. Gordon had lied. When her husband had come to her hospital-room with tears in his eyes, to tell her Natalie hadn't survived the car crash as she had, he had lied. He had left her wanting to die too, for her daughter was the one thing she loved best in the world. Knowing it, Gordon had used it against her. Taking their daughter from her, and leaving her to six years of guilt and grief.

It was almost beyond belief, yet she believed it of him. She knew him too well. He had taken Natalie, not because he wanted her himself, but simply so that she, Claudia, could not have her. For as long as she lived she would never forgive him for that.

She looked up, and suddenly it occurred to her that something didn't quite fit. 'What made Gordon change his mind?' she asked, voice sharp with suspicion.

'Gordon?' Tyler looked and sounded surprised.

Feeling at a distinct disadvantage, Claudia swung her feet cautiously to the floor and stood up. The world, thankfully, stayed put. Her brain was ticking over fast. 'There has to be a reason. Six years ago he told me Natalie was dead. Now he's sent you here to tell me she's alive. Why?' To turn the screw in some sadistic way?

'Gordon didn't send me here, or anywhere. He died in a plane crash six months ago.'

'Six months ago!' Claudia reeled from this latest discovery.

Tyler's eyes narrowed. 'There's no need to act so surprised. I wrote and told you months ago.'

She knew then what had happened, could see in her mind the unopened package of private mail resting on her desk. She hadn't been home here for months, and, having only arrived days ago, hadn't yet got around to opening her correspondence. 'I've seen no letter. I've not been here in ages. It's probably on my desk, but... Natalie. Who's been looking after her?'

'Natalie is living with me,' Tyler informed her levelly. 'Gordon appointed me her guardian.'

Claudia wasn't just shocked that in death Gordon had still managed to have his own way, she was stunned, and her eyes glittered with disbelieving anger. 'He gave her to you? She's *my* daughter. I'm her mother, for God's sake! I had the right to have her!' she choked out thickly.

Tyler's lips curled scornfully. 'Isn't this concern six years too late? If you wanted Natalie you should have applied for custody at the time of the divorce. Which we both know you didn't do. All you were interested in was the money and how soon it could be passed over! You never even mentioned Natalie. What sort of mother is it who abandons her baby?'

That tore at her heart. At the time of the divorce she had just wanted the marriage over. All she had done was instruct her lawyers not to contest and simply pay over the amount agreed at the time of her marriage. As for Natalie... 'I didn't abandon her. How could I apply for custody of a child I didn't know existed? I told you what Gordon said. You've got to believe me!'

His face shut down. 'Why? Why should I believe a woman who lies about being married? Who breaks all the vows she made in her search for excitement? Those things *I* know to be true, Claudia, don't I? Whatever lies you made up to justify your actions, they mean nothing to me. You've lied and cheated for the last time, because *I* know you for what you are.'

The words hit her like blows, and, ashen-faced, she turned away. He wouldn't believe her because she *had* lied to him. He wouldn't let her explain then, as he wouldn't listen now. And any chance that she might have had had been destroyed by her own actions these last six years. She had transgressed, and it didn't matter to him why. The act had been enough. It was something he would never forgive.

She had accepted that a long time ago. She wouldn't beg. If he ever did ask then she would tell him. Until then there was nothing she could do, but she could fight for her daughter. After six lost years nobody was going to stop her.

Claudia turned, face stamped with a determination that had been missing so long. 'I want to see her,' she stated firmly. 'I want to see her, Tyler. *Now.*'

He didn't look amused. 'It isn't going to be as easy as that.'

Her hands clenched into fists at her sides. 'You mean you aren't going to let me see her?' She'd see about that! She had her rights!

'I didn't say that. I said it wasn't going to be easy. Natalie isn't with me. I left her in England.'

'In England?' Her surprise was dampened by a sudden unpalatable thought. 'With your wife?'

Tyler's lips curled. 'I'm not married, Claudia, if that's what you wanted to know. I left Natalie in hospital.'

'Hospital!' Claudia collapsed on to the nearest chair. 'Oh, my God! What is it? What's happened?' She had visions of losing Natalie before she'd even found her again. And all the time Tyler was watching her with those calculating eyes, testing her every reaction for honesty. Dear lord, what did he think she was? Scrap the question. She already knew what he thought, and it was irrelevant. Natalie was all that mattered now. Life had become worth living again, and she wasn't going to let anything come in the way of that.

So she bit back an automatic retort. 'Tell me,' she ordered hardily, bracing herself.

Tyler stiffened too, showing her that he wasn't inhuman. That what he had to say was hard for him. It gave her a crazy feeling of warmth to know that he must love her daughter very much.

'Natalie has a heart condition. It was thought that she would always be an invalid, but now, thanks to new technology, there's an operation she can have to put it right. It's common enough, but it is major heart surgery. There's always an element of risk. Natalie knows that but she's willing to take the gamble.'

Claudia pressed a hand over her mouth, afraid she would cry out. A violent tremble had seized her. 'When?'

A muscle jerked in his jaw. 'Tomorrow.'

Claudia closed her eyes. 'So soon?' What if it went wrong? What if she never got to see her daughter again? Why hadn't he come sooner? Why had he left it so late?

It was almost as if Tyler could read her mind.

'I hadn't intended to come at all. You'd made your feelings about Natalie perfectly clear. However, much as you may dislike it, Natalie *is* your daughter. You had a right to know what was happening. What you choose to do now is entirely up to you.' The note he ended on made it perfectly clear what he thought she would do.

It hurt to know she had sunk so low in his estimation. Her lips twisted bitterly. 'So it's your conscience I have to thank for your being here. It can't have been easy for you, consorting with the likes of me. You should have used the telephone. Much more antiseptic.'

'This sort of news is not for the telephone. It has to be face to face, even if that means seeing you again, Claudia. And now I'll have to be going.' He glanced at the gold Rolex on his wrist. 'My flight leaves in three hours. I don't want to miss it. I promised Natalie I would see her tonight.'

Claudia was on her feet at once. 'I'm coming with you,' she declared. She didn't need time to think. As soon as she had known Natalie was alive there was only one place for her to be.

Tyler paused mid-stride. 'You needn't put yourself to so much trouble. Nobody expects it.'

It was a deliberate slap in the face, but she weathered it. 'Perhaps they don't, but I do. Believe what you like, Tyler, but I've always loved my daughter. I've been kept from her too long, and I won't waste another precious moment. So, if you won't take me with you, I'll go alone. I intend to be with her, and I will,' Claudia stated firmly, standing her ground.

There was a strange, calculating look in his eye. 'Are you sure you want to do this? Because if you come I won't allow you to back out.'

Was he warning her of something she didn't know? Her heart knocked, but there was no room for doubts. 'I'm coming,' she insisted.

He was silent a moment before slowly inclining his head. 'Very well. You'd better go and throw a few things together while I arrange for another ticket. I'll be leaving in fifteen minutes if you're ready or not.'

The threat didn't daunt her. 'I'll be ready,' she assured him as she hurried from the room, calling for Seraphina as she ran up the stairs. Only one thing mattered: she was going to see Natalie. It didn't matter what Tyler or anyone else thought of her. She was going to her daughter, and that made up for everything.

CHAPTER TWO

As THE huge jet reached its cruising altitude Claudia relaxed back in her seat with an exhausted sigh. There was nothing to do now but sit and wait. The last couple of hours had been hectic. Seraphina had helped her pack while she'd showered and changed into white cotton trousers and a scarlet silk shirt. She had had to write a note for her aunt too. There hadn't been time for long explanations, but she promised to telephone as soon as she had time.

Tyler had observed her reappearance in under fifteen minutes with a mocking smile, but for the moment she'd refused to let it get at her. She had sat beside him in silence as he'd taken the *autostrada* to the nearest airport, keeping to the maximum speed limit. She hadn't attempted to distract him, but that wasn't because of any fault with his driving. Simply that she too had wanted the journey to be over, though perhaps for different reasons.

Now, though, they had a flight of several hours ahead of them, with too much time to think. Beside her, Tyler was making himself comfortable, stretching out his long legs in the spacious first-class compartment. He had been courteous and helpful through all the formalities, but she suspected that that was because it had been expedient to do so.

She was under no illusion, yet she remembered him as a naturally charming and courteous man. But she had forfeited all that when he'd discovered the truth about her.

'Why don't you try and sleep?' Tyler suggested, making her start, her thoughts miles away.

Claudia shook her head. 'I couldn't possibly.'

He shrugged, quickly losing interest, and closed his eyes. 'Suit yourself. I intend to. This is the second flight I've made in just a few hours. I didn't sleep much last night either.' Within seconds she could hear his steady breathing.

She wondered what he would say if she told him she, too, was suffering the effects of jet lag. Nothing probably. Studying him closely, Claudia could see his fatigue in the slight grey cast to his skin. He didn't show it, but he was just as worried as she. More so, probably, because he had lived with it longer. How she envied him that worry. A lump rose in her throat and tears burnt the backs of her eyes.

So much. She had missed so much. How could Gordon have done that?

What a question! Easily, was the answer. For Gordon Peterson such vindictiveness was second nature.

Tyler stirred, making himself more comfortable in his sleep, and she jumped as she felt his head come to rest on her shoulder. Automatically she lifted a hand to push him away, then hesitated. Looking down at him, seeing the ruffled black hair, the splay of long lashes upon bruised cheeks, she bit her lip. It was so long since he had been this close to her. She could smell the spicy tang of his aftershave, and the subtle scent that was peculiar to him alone. Her heart twisted.

She shouldn't let him stay there. It was madness. If he woke and found out he'd be furious. Yet he was so very tired. A stray lock of hair had fallen across his brow, and her fingers tingled with the urge to brush it back. She fought it, curling her fingers into her palm. It was foolish to taunt herself with the impossible. She looked away from him, staring blindly out of the window, willing herself to ignore how his closeness made her feel. She would always be his, but he would never be hers. Too much stood between them. More, even, than she had supposed.

She shuddered in a chill of memories that rushed back. She didn't want to recall anything, but she had no control over it. Her brain projected the events of her past on to the screen of her consciousness, and she was the helpless spectator.

With hindsight Claudia knew that at eighteen she had been unbelievably naïve, and marrying Gordon Peterson had been the greatest folly. Only it hadn't seemed like folly at the time. It had been a bid for independence, and at the same time a reaching out for the love and affection that had been missing from her life. She had reached for a dream, only to have it shattered by reality. There had been no going back after that.

Her upbringing had been a recipe for disaster. She barely remembered her parents. They had died young, in the same accident that had robbed her cousin Amelia of her own parents. Both girls had been placed in the guardianship of their elderly uncles. Claudia had only known her American relatives because her Italian mother had been disowned by her family for defying them to marry Matthew Webster. The Websters were old money, and, although Matthew was the younger son, at four years old Claudia had found herself the heiress to a moderate fortune, and living in a huge mansion in New York.

The mansion and the real fortune were Amelia's, but, even so, the two girls were generally known as the Webster heiresses. Their guardians—in actuality their great-uncles—knew a great deal about money, but very little about young children. They did know their wards had a position to fill, and they were educated for it by a series of governesses followed by a select finishing school. It was a stifling, rarefied atmosphere for any child, let alone one with a Latin temperament. While Amelia seemed almost to thrive on it, Claudia longed to escape the claustrophobic confines of their lives, where their friends were carefully chosen for them, and they were trained to do nothing but be who they were—the Webster heiresses.

However kindly they were, her great-uncles were dinosaurs. Her pleas to be allowed to do something useful with her life they found bewildering. When once she asked to be given a job with the family business they laughed. Nobody understood her, not even the easygoing Amelia. The concept of a woman—especially a Webster—'working' was frowned upon. The fact that she had inherited a keen mind and a lively intelligence from her father was neither here nor there. Whatever plan she put forward they vetoed, leaving her frustrated and alienated.

Then, during a long weekend in Rhode Island, she met Gordon Peterson. He flattered her with his attentions and, emotionally starved all her life, with a desperate need to love and be loved, she had been swept off her feet by the handsome Englishman. When she told her great-uncles she intended to marry him they were aghast. She refused to listen when they called him an adventurer and a fortune hunter. She wanted Gordon and they couldn't stop her because she was over eighteen by then.

They had been forced to capitulate, but they had taken the precaution of drawing up a marriage contract. Brought up on such formalities, and relieved not to have had a harder fight, she had seen nothing wrong, but Gordon had been furious, accusing her of doubting his honour. She should have been warned then, but instead she had soothed him anxiously, explaining that it was only a formality, and had breathed a sigh of relief when he had relented and signed.

The wedding had taken place in a blaze of publicity. The guests had numbered hundreds. It was a glittering day, filled with happiness and excitement. It was hard to believe how eagerly she had gone off on their honeymoon to the Seychelles. The setting was idyllic, but oh, how swiftly the idyll had turned sour. Her wedding-night had opened her eyes to many things.

At first their lovemaking was perfect, all she'd expected it to be. Gordon's kisses and caresses had slowly dissolved the nervous tension of her untried body. But she was nowhere near ready for him when he rolled her on to her back and parted her thighs with his. She had been prepared for some discomfort, but not the painful initiation that followed. Her own fledgling arousal quite gone, she had tried to make him stop, to wait because he was hurting her, but Gordon had been too intent on reaching his own pleasure. She had lain beneath him, biting her lip to stop herself from crying out. When it was over, and he rolled off her with a mumbled, 'Fantastic,' before falling asleep, she only felt sick and betrayed.

At first she had made excuses for his insensitivity, telling herself he hadn't really meant to hurt her, but by the end of the honeymoon she had stopped pretending. Her rose-coloured glasses lay smashed. The man she'd married didn't exist, had never existed outside her own lonely dreams. Gordon was a selfish man and a selfish lover. He gave no thought to her pleasure, only his own. When she complained that he was hurting her he became blazingly angry. Nobody had ever complained before, he had shouted at her, telling her that if anyone was at fault it was her. She was frigid. It was like taking a lump of ice to bed.

Any love she had felt had died a rapid death, and in the unblinkered light at last she had begun to doubt his feelings for her. She would never forget the moment when, lying bruised and aching beside him after he had taken his pleasure, Gordon had called her a frigid bitch, and she had finally asked him why he had married her.

His answer had flayed her pride.

'Because, darling, you're Claudia Webster. You're a walking cash register, and you're all mine. You're beautiful, but that's a bonus. Frankly, you could look like the back of a bus, and I'd still have married you. All I'd have to do is think of all that money—it's a powerful aphrodisiac.' He laughed. 'See what I mean? Come here, Claudia, and for God's sake put a bit of life into it!'

The truth had hurt as it was meant to do, but even as she'd lain there, biting back tears, her pride had surfaced. Although she now loathed Gordon, nothing in the world would make her run home and admit she had been wrong. Nobody made a fool of a Webster, not

visibly, anyway. Pride she hadn't even realised she had made her raise her chin and put
on a brave face. She had made a mistake but
she wanted no pity, no smug smiles and
knowing looks. Anything was better than
that. Even marriage to Gordon.

Her relief when the honeymoon was over
and they flew home to England was
enormous. She soon found she could be
almost happy there. Gordon's work took him
away all day, leaving her to breathe new life
into the house and grounds. She might even
have been content if Gordon had left her
alone. But his passion for her hadn't dimin-
ished, despite her growing lack of response,
and she found that degrading.

She had known it was only a matter of time
before he asked about the money, and one day
he had come home with grandiose plans for
buying up land near by and turning it into an
exclusive club. Calmly she had enquired how
much cash he needed, and been staggered by
the amount he stated.

'I don't have that sort of money,' she had
told him simply, and he had laughed.

'Come off it, the Websters are millionaires.'

She had felt sick. 'But not me. All I have
is a few thousand, and that's held in trust for
me until I'm twenty-one.'

Gordon's face had turned ugly. 'You're trying to trick me. Don't think I didn't check that you were older than your cousin.'

By now Claudia was shaking with distaste. 'You didn't check enough. Yes, I'm older than Amelia, but my father was the younger son. You married the wrong Webster. Amelia's the heiress, not me.' There had been a wealth of satisfaction in telling him that. A much-needed salve to her wounded pride.

His anger had been of the spiteful, vindictive kind. She hadn't seen him for days, and then when he had returned he had begun a string of affairs. Affairs he had never troubled to hide from her. When she had complained, his handsome face had been distorted by a sneer.

'If you don't like it why don't you run back to your family?' he had taunted. 'But you've too much pride for that, haven't you, Claudia? Poor little Claudia, whom nobody loves!'

Her pride, which had taken so much, would take no more. Instead of licking her wounds, she had rebelled. Why should she stay married to a man she loathed and who constantly abused her verbally and physically? Only a sense of false pride had kept her loyal. Weakly she had let him win, but now she discovered a strength and determination that had lain dormant within her. She needed not take it, and she wouldn't. She would divorce Gordon and make a new life for herself.

Yet it would take careful planning. She didn't think Gordon would let her go easily. She would have to think it through, and she couldn't do that there. When she had told him she was going on holiday he hadn't made a fuss and she had known that that must be because there was a new woman in his life.

She had gone to Italy. Long ago, among her mother's papers, she had discovered who her Italian relatives were, and had contacted her mother's sister. Her Aunt Lucia had welcomed her warmly, noticing at once the absence of Claudia's wedding-ring, which she had removed even before the plane had left Heathrow. She had asked no questions, only listened when Claudia had finally wanted to talk.

Confiding to someone who cared about her had lifted a great weight from her mind. Claudia had had no doubts. Divorce was the right, the only thing to do. In fact, in leaving England she had already left him. When she got back she would collect her belongings and move out.

Relaxed in body and spirit, she had begun to explore the beautiful Italian countryside, and that was when she had met Tyler. It had been during a visit to some Roman ruins. They had quite literally bumped into each other. She would always remember that moment; it had been quite incredible. As he reached out to steady her the sun had seemed to shine twice as brightly. The birdsong had been piercingly sweet and the scents of the wild flowers had intoxicated her—and he had felt it too. It was there in the stunned look in his eyes.

Then they had both backed off. Just fighting free of the shackles of a disastrous marriage, Claudia didn't know if she was ready for what her emotions were telling her. It was too soon. And yet, over the next few days, they had seemed to keep meeting each other in the most unlikely places. She would nod and he would respond, and, though no words were spoken, somehow she sensed he was pleased to see her. She had certainly felt the same about him.

Eventually a nod had become hello, hello a polite exchange of knowledge, until one day Tyler invited her to have coffee, and she had smiled and he returned it, and the whole world had changed in those seconds. They had spent that day together, and those following, talking incessantly. He had told her he was a financial consultant, a trouble-shooter, and that he was on an extended holiday. She had simply said she was on holiday too, for it had seemed simpler at the time. They seemed to have so much to say, and by the end of the week she had felt she had known him all her life. She also knew she had fallen in love, really in love, and that whatever she felt, Tyler felt it too.

They had spent every available minute together, the attraction they felt for each other growing in intensity. From the first kiss they had shared the fires of passion had burned fiercely, but, as if by mutual agreement, they did not rush to consummate it. There was an inevitability about their feelings that made it unnecessary. One day they would make love, and it would be perfect; until then just to be with each other was a joy to be savoured.

Love, mutually confessed, surrounded them like a glow.

One day they had decided to picnic along the coast. Nothing had given her any warning of what was to come: that her world could come falling about her ears like a house of cards. They had eaten, and she was resting against Tyler, glancing through a magazine, when she had felt him tense; then his hand had come out to flick back the page to where a picture of a smiling man and woman stood out. She was in her early fifties. Strikingly beautiful, her dark hair just showing the strands of grey at the temples. He was a good ten years older, not technically handsome, but with a shock of white hair. The caption read, 'Will it be third time lucky for Nancy? She deserves it, and our hearts go out to her.'

'My God!' The words had exploded from him.

Startled, Claudia had looked from the picture to Tyler, alarmed by the coldness in his eyes. 'Who are they?'

'I don't know who he is, but she's my ever-loving mother!'

To say she had been shocked was an understatement. But Tyler hadn't finished yet. 'Women like her deserve nothing but contempt!'

'What did she do?' Though she wasn't able to say why, Claudia's heart had taken up an anxious beating.

'Do? She broke every vow and every promise that ever came from those sweet lying lips. She walked out when I was ten years old. She swore she'd never leave, but she just left one day and never came back,' Tyler growled as he clambered to his feet.

The change in him was staggering. Claudia stood up too. 'But why? There had to be a reason.'

His jaw clenched. 'Because she was faithless. Because her vows meant nothing to her. I have nothing but contempt for her and every woman like her!'

Claudia's blood went cold. She took a very shaky breath, choosing her words carefully. 'Are you saying a woman should stay married to a man, whatever the cost? Surely there are circumstances —— ?'

'None!' he interrupted her brutally. 'To me vows are sacred. Marriage is forever. Women who betray that are worthless. I've never played with a married woman, Claudia, and I would never forgive those married women who chase men.'

She was shaking by then, yet she was forced to go on. 'That's a very...black and white attitude. Life isn't that simple, Tyler.'

'To me it is.'

Desperately she tried to discover a softening in him so that what she had to say would be easier, but there was none. She couldn't believe what was happening. 'What if I were married, Tyler?' she queried softly.

He didn't say she was different; instead his eyes dropped to her hand. 'You aren't wearing any rings.'

Automatically her other hand covered where hers had so recently lain. 'I could have taken them off,' she went on huskily, and felt his narrowed gaze like a knife. The very air about them had seemed to stop moving.

'What are you saying, Claudia?'

Every instinct urged her to stop, but she knew she couldn't. 'I'm asking you a question. I love you and you love me. If I told you I were married, what then?'

Nothing moved around them, and his words fell like lead weights. 'Then it would be over.'

'Just like that?'

'Exactly like that. You might not like it, but that's the way it is. Now I'd rather forget I ever saw——'

'I'm married, Tyler.' Her bald statement cut him off.

'What?' His face went white. 'What did you say?'

Somehow she held herself together. 'I said I'm married. I was going to tell you——'

It was his turn to cut in. 'When? When you'd made a fool of me? My God, you little liar!'

She grabbed his arm then. 'Tyler, let me explain.'

He shrugged her off, eyes as remote as the Arctic wastes. 'There's nothing to say I want to hear. Get your things—we're leaving.'

And that had been that. He hadn't said another word to her on that long ride home. He had dropped her off at the villa and hadn't looked back as he drove away. She hadn't been able to believe it could end so swiftly. Worst of all was knowing that Tyler loved her but had rejected her without a hearing.

It had been Aunt Lucia, listening to Claudia's heartbroken story, who had offered a ray of hope. '*Caro*, let him cool down. He's angry now. Call him tonight and explain.'

It had seemed sound advice, but when she had tried it she had been told that Tyler had gone and left no forwarding address.

Her emotions had gone into a kind of limbo, a deep freeze. Yet she had returned home even more determined to get a divorce. Because, if she had learned nothing else from her short while with Tyler, she had learned what true love was. Unrequited it might be, but anything less would be intolerable.

Yet nothing had gone quite the way she had planned because she was greeted by a vastly changed Gordon. Gone was the churlish womaniser, and in his place was a very warm and considerate husband. His contrition stopped her in her tracks. He told her how her absence had made him do some thinking. How he realised things hadn't been right between them of late, but that he thought they should try to save their marriage.

When she didn't immediately reject the idea—because she hadn't decided quite what to make of it—Gordon had seen it as a good sign and started to wine and dine her. He had bought her red roses and jewellery, and kept her so off balance by his attentiveness that one evening, when he had been particularly charming, he had coaxed her, against her better judgement, into making love.

Her resolve had wavered a little then, and she had let matters drift. Things were much better than they had ever been during their marriage. Then she had discovered she was pregnant. Her feelings were mixed. She had always wanted a child, but not that Gordon would be the father. Quite what she would have done she didn't know, but a letter had arrived that pulled the wool from her eyes.

It was from her cousin Amelia, saying that she had had a remission and that her doctors were hopeful of a full recovery in time. She had read the letter out at breakfast and Gordon had exploded. He had cursed her cousin and sneered at her own confusion.

'Damn all you Websters,' he said nastily. 'You can't even die when you're supposed to! Hell, I could almost taste the money!' He laughed at her dawning comprehension. 'That's right, I knew she was dying. Her letter came while you were away. Why the hell else do you think I was being so "nice", darling?'

From that moment on he reverted back to his old self. With no prospect of money, he didn't even bother to pretend. Claudia was left knowing that twice she had fallen for his lies, but it made her determined that there would never be a third time. Yet there was the baby to consider now. For that reason alone she felt she had to stay with Gordon. She knew what it was like to be without parents, and she wanted her child to have a proper stable background.

Time had passed. Natalie had brought joy into her life from the day she came screaming into the world. She had been as happy as she ever expected to be. She had tried not to think of Tyler and what might have been, putting him into the past because she never expected to see him again.

Only she had. When Natalie was about a year old, Claudia and Gordon had gone to a family anniversary party—and the very first person she had seen was Tyler. She had still been struggling with the knowledge when Gordon made the introductions.

'Tyler, old man, I don't think you know my wife, Claudia. Darling, this here's my cousin from Africa. We met up at Oxford years ago.'

Afterwards she was never able to remember what she said; all she had been aware of was the contemptuous glitter in Tyler's eyes as he shook her hand and then made his excuses.

He had left soon after, while she had had to fend off Gordon's mocking comments that she had driven him away.

Seeing Tyler had left her devastated, unable to hate him or stop loving him. Into this melting-pot Gordon had indicated a wish to share her bed again. That she hadn't been prepared to allow. Her refusal was blunt, and Gordon's reaction terrifying. She had never seen him so angry as he was then. The things he had said, the names he had called her, were vicious. Disgusted and angry, she had made the error of ordering him out of her room. She had only realised the enormity of that mistake when he had grabbed her and forced her down on to the bed. The degradation of what had followed had been the last straw for her.

She had left the next day, taking Natalie with her. She had had no destination in mind, only a determination not to stay there a day longer.

Yet, even there, fate had been against her, for a tyre had blown on the motorway. She had spent two weeks in Intensive Care after the crash. When she had awoken that first time in a private room Gordon had been there. A Gordon who, with tears in his eyes, told her Natalie was dead. She had been crazy with grief. Guilt had pounded into her with every beat of her heart. She was responsible for Natalie's death, for if she had stayed her daughter would still be alive.

Racked by it, she had fled to her Aunt Lucia as soon as she was fit enough to travel. She hadn't cared when Gordon sued for divorce, simply ordering her lawyer to settle as their marriage contract demanded, though it had taken nearly all her inheritance. She hadn't cared about anything.

The ultimate irony had come only days later. She had learned that her cousin had died, making her, Claudia, the Webster heiress after all. It hardly mattered. In a desperate attempt to forget she had thrown herself into a reckless lifestyle that was totally out of character. Doing crazy, wild things in search of oblivion. At first she had numbered it in hours only. Gradually time had been kind, healing the wound until it was bearable.

Claudia came back from the past with a shiver. All those wasted years believing Natalie was dead! Only a mind as sick as Gordon's could have put her through that. But it was over now. He could no longer keep them apart. And she had Tyler, of all people, to thank for that.

Even in the distorted image reflected by the window her eyes shone. At last, after so long a parting, she was going to see Natalie. She tried to conjure up those first few moments, but no image would come. Natalie had been little more than a year old when last she had seen her, and, no matter how she tried, she couldn't picture her now, at nearly eight.

A shadow passed across her face. Lord, she wouldn't even recognise her own daughter! Another thought followed: would Natalie know her? Would she be pleased to see her mother? Her stomach knotted painfully. What had Gordon told her? Claudia chewed on her lip nervously. In those years what picture could he have painted? The possibilities open to his vindictive mind were limitless. What if he...? Oh, God, snap out of it! You'll drive yourself crazy this way, she told herself sharply. Wait and see. Take each problem as it arises. That was all she could do. Whatever Gordon had done, time was on her side now.

A long-drawn-out sigh drew her startled eyes sideways to encounter sleepy blue ones. Somewhat hysterically she realised she had forgotten Tyler completely. Now he was awake and lifting his head from her shoulder with a sharp narrowing of his eyes.

'You should have woken me,' he said shortly, straightening up.

Claudia sighed, smoothing her jacket where he had rested. 'You were tired and my shoulder was free. Don't worry, your integrity hasn't been compromised.' She watched as he stretched, her eyes drawn to the flexing muscles of his thighs, seeing the strength there. Leashed strength that was part of the whole man she had known so briefly. Her mouth went dry. Beautiful memories assaulted her, and she banished them with an effort. To want Tyler was to want the moon and the stars, and they were as unattainable as his love and respect.

'Don't go getting any ideas of starting up where you left off, Claudia,' Tyler declared harshly, and she glanced up, hot colour storming her cheeks as she realised he had been watching her. 'I wouldn't soil my hands on someone who's been round the course as often as you have.'

All colour fled as swiftly as it had come. 'You don't have to try so hard to insult me, Tyler. The ''off-limit'' signs were posted a long time ago, and I wouldn't dream of overstepping the mark. All I'm interested in is Natalie.' Even as she said it she knew it wasn't true, but there was a vast chasm between what she wanted and what she knew she could have. She knew she ought to hate him for what he had done, but it just wasn't in her. You couldn't love to order, and you couldn't hate either.

'So interested that you ignored her existence for six years.'

'How easy it is for you to condemn me! What a loyal champion Gordon had in you!' Claudia declared bitterly, eyes holding his. 'I told you he lied to me. He told me Natalie was dead. One of us is lying, and you choose to believe it's me. Because that fits in with your black and white view of the world. But you're forgetting something, Tyler. Gordon used people. He preyed on their weaknesses. What you see as a strength was a weakness to him, something to be exploited. And that's precisely what he's done. Right this minute I don't know who I feel sorry for most—you or me!'

Tyler's face was tight with anger. 'Keep your pity for yourself; I don't need it.'

Claudia shook her head sadly. 'Oh, Tyler, what you need you won't allow yourself to have. You've got to learn to have compassion for human frailty, not contempt.'

He uttered a harsh bark of laughter. 'Coming from you, that's priceless!'

She should have known she was wasting her time, but she had had to try, for his sake. 'I'd like to meet your mother,' she said flatly.

His head shot round. 'What the hell for?'

Claudia reached for her bag and stood up. 'To compare notes, of course. I think we have a lot in common. Far more than your narrow vision will ever see. Excuse me, I'm going to freshen up.' Pushing past his legs, she stepped into the aisle, heading for the nearest toilet and the relative sanctuary it represented.

Locking herself inside, she rested her hot forehead against the blessedly cool mirror. Why on earth was she bothering? Why couldn't she simply be content with having Natalie restored to her? Because she still loved him, of course. And loving meant that you helped that person with no expectations of gain for yourself. Certainly she expected nothing, but there was a tiny corner of her heart that still hoped, despite everything.

Crazy it certainly was, and hopeless. Yet Natalie's return had been even more hopeless until today. So it behoved her to tread softly where Tyler was concerned. She must learn to co-exist with him, to weather his attitude as best she could. He had fallen a victim to Gordon's lies just as she had. Proving it would be next to impossible, but, even so, she knew she was going to try.

She smiled wryly to herself. Which only went to show it wasn't only blondes who were dumb!

Just then somebody knocked on the door, reminding her that she was monopolising the room. Claudia quickly wiped her face with a damp paper towel, restored her make-up with a few deft touches, and let herself out, smiling an apology to the young woman waiting outside.

When she rejoined Tyler it was to find he had removed his jacket during her absence. He had also ordered them both coffee. She realised then that she was actually quite thirsty, having had nothing since breakfast. So her thanks were quite genuine as she sat down beside him. He said nothing though, and they sat in silence for a while, sipping at the refreshing liquid.

Her thoughts naturally turned to her daughter. There were so many questions. So many things she didn't know. So much wasted time to make up for. Yet only one question was so vital that it had her twisting round in her seat to face her silent companion.

'Tyler.' Her husky voice drew his attention.

'What?'

The sharpness of his tone made her wince and subside back into her seat. Lord, he was so cold! 'It doesn't matter. Forget it,' she murmured, keeping her eyes on the clouds outside.

Tyler sighed long-sufferingly. 'Claudia, I don't have time for your games. Just ask me what you were going to ask.'

Her hands tightened on the cup, wishing she hadn't started now that she was forced to go on. 'I wondered...what does she look like?' There, it was out now, and she waited for his scornful reply.

Clearly he hadn't been expecting that particular question, for he remained silent for some time. So long, in fact, that Claudia had come to believe he wasn't going to answer at all, when he said, 'She has her hair in one of those long plaits.'

Her eyes flew to his face. 'She has long hair, then?' she asked eagerly.

There was mockery in his gaze as he viewed her enthusiasm, but his words were gentle. 'She persuaded Wendy—that's her nanny— to let her grow her hair long.'

'She had such lovely thick brown hair,' Claudia murmured reminiscently. 'Is it...?'

'Still the same,' he agreed wryly, eyes watching her changing expressions inscrutably. 'Her eyes are sort of hazel. Her nose tilts up, which she hates, and has freckles. She hates those too. Her skin is lighter than yours, and very fine. She's going to be a stunner, mark my words!'

Claudia gave a choked laugh, eyes and lips smiling. 'Is she?'

Tyler's look became brooding. 'She takes after you. I can't see much of Gordon in her.'

She gave a tiny sigh. 'Surely you don't hold that against her?' she asked.

'Of course not!' he returned smoothly. 'It's not her fault who her mother is. That was an accident of birth. She's an innocent, and I intend to make sure she stays that way.'

'Meaning?'

'Meaning don't think you can simply walk back into her life and take it over,' he warned coldly.

Claudia met that look squarely. 'She's my daughter, Tyler. I refuse to be a stranger to her any more,' she countered firmly. 'What have you told her about me?'

His smile was grim. 'Not a word.'

Claudia's heart skipped a beat. 'I don't believe you. She must have asked about me.'

One eyebrow rose mockingly. 'Never in my hearing, or even to my knowledge. I'm afraid that, as far as Natalie is concerned, you don't even exist!'

CHAPTER THREE

IT WAS almost dusk when they touched down at Heathrow. Though it was summer, it had been raining, and the night had drawn in early. The heavy air only served to deepen Claudia's own personal cloud. Her tension had mounted the nearer they came to their destination, the situation not helped by Tyler's statement. They had hardly exchanged a word since, and she had been left to her own unhappy thoughts. Knowing Natalie hadn't shown any interest in her absent mother filled Claudia with foreboding. She wasn't prepared for this meeting, and a thousand and one 'what if's clamoured in her head.

It was a relief to land and have something else to think about. Airport formalities were mercifully swift for a change, and in a very short time they were on their way again, Tyler's hand firmly fixed about her arm as he steered her towards the exit.

'My car's in the short-stay car park,' he informed her, striding out so that both she and

58

the porter carrying her luggage were almost forced to trot to keep up.

'Will it take long to get there?'

'Not at this time of night.' Tyler reached his car, a comfortable saloon, and released her in order to tip the porter. 'There's no restriction on visiting, but I thought we'd go straight to the hospital, unless you want to go to my hotel and change first?' His tone suggested he had little doubt she'd choose the latter option.

Claudia watched him stack her cases in the boot, aware that she was starting to feel sick with nerves. She found herself torn between the two conflicting emotions of impatience and reluctance. 'Natalie will be expecting you, won't she?' She dragged a hand through her hair and managed a tense smile. 'It doesn't matter what I look like. It's not fair to get her worried so close to her operation.' Did she imagine a brief look of approval before he held open the passenger-door?

'The hospital it is, then.'

Seconds later, with practised ease, Tyler steered the large car out into the London-bound traffic. It started to rain again and Claudia followed the motion of the wind-screen-wipers, sensing them ticking away the seconds. If only Tyler would show some warmth and allow her to share her anxiety, but his concentration was total, and she was left once more to her own devices. Her mind dreamed up various scenarios for the meeting ahead, but they all fled as they finally reached the hospital. He parked the car, and in no time at all she was following him into the imposing building on trembling legs.

The moment was upon her now. There was only a short lift ride and a walk and then she would be at Natalie's room. As the lift doors closed her heart failed her. How could she possibly cope? Was she doing the right thing, or was she being selfish? Natalie wasn't expecting her. Surely it would have been better to wait until after the operation?

The lift stopped. The die had been cast. More scared than she had ever been in her life before, she followed Tyler mechanically, heart thudding. He halted outside a door and turned to look at her. His eyes probed hers. As he saw her anxiety his expression softened a little.

'Natalie doesn't know you're coming. You'd better wait out here while I tell her,' he said gruffly.

Claudia nodded and swallowed, unable to find her voice, yet grateful for his consideration. Tyler hesitated only a moment longer before passing through the door, letting it close slowly behind him. On her own, Claudia could hear the gentle murmur of his voice, and, answering it, a young girl's childish treble. Her heart contracted painfully in her chest at the sound, and she felt weak. Without any conscious volition she felt the wood of the door against her palm, stopping its closure. She was drawn to the sound of that voice like a magnet. In the doorway she paused, her eyes travelling to the bed.

There were three people there. A young woman in her early twenties, wearing a neat print dress, stood to one side of the bed. Tyler was sitting on the edge of it, bending over the slight form of a young girl. Natalie!

Claudia drew in a long, painfully ragged breath, trying not to cry or make a sound as she gazed at her daughter at long last. Anguish tore her heart apart. Dear heaven, she looked so young, so fragile and vulnerable—and so very, very beautiful. Tyler was right about her face, and the freckles. Yet there was nothing of the baby she remembered. Gordon had robbed her of all those growing years. She didn't know her. She's not my baby any more, her heart wept. She's a stranger. A stranger who possessed the power to destroy her mother more easily than she could ever know.

Even as she thought it her arms ached to sweep her daughter into them, to hold her tight and never let her go. To banish the emptiness she had felt for six long years. Only Natalie could fill that void.

The compulsion to act was so strong that she had taken a step into the room before she realised. Three pairs of eyes turned in her direction. There was a moment of shocked surprise, and then Tyler was at her side in an instant.

He frowned heavily, taking her arm. 'I thought I told you to wait,' he spat at her.

Claudia barely spared him a glance. 'I couldn't. Please don't ask me to.'

Tyler swore and stepped in front of her. 'Claudia —— '

'Is that her?'

The cool little voice interrupted what Tyler might have said. For a moment there was indecision on his face, then, shrugging fatalistically, he stood aside. Claudia found herself being surveyed by an unwavering unfriendly pair of eyes. They made her shiver with their remoteness, and before panic could set in she forced a smile to her lips and approached the bed.

'Hello, Natalie.' Her voice was an emotive croak as all sorts of emotions assailed her at once. Quickly she bent to kiss her daughter, and found that cheek pointedly removed. It was like having a stake driven through her heart, and she blanched, gasping at the pain of it. She straightened stiffly, throat working madly on a lump that restricted her breathing.

The impassive little face stared back at her. 'Are you really my mother?' she asked incuriously.

Hastily gathering her scattered wits, Claudia nodded. 'Yes, I really am.'

'In that case you ought to know that all Daddy's money is mine now. Tyler looks after it for me, don't you?' she appealed to her guardian.

Tyler frowned heavily. 'You know I do, poppet, but this is hardly the time or place to talk about it,' he reproved gently.

Natalie's eyes widened. 'But it is. She has to know that, because it's what she came for!' the young girl protested, turning her gaze to where her mother stood in stricken silence. 'That's true, isn't it?'

Claudia's eyes flew to Tyler in mute appeal before dropping to her daughter again. 'No, it isn't. I came to see *you*, Natalie. Why— why would you think I wanted your money?'

The question issued from a painfully tight throat.

'Because Daddy said you'd come back one day, but only when you wanted some money.'

Claudia was appalled. 'But that's not true!' she exclaimed, staring with disbelief at the closed little face. 'I came because I love you.'

Natalie shrugged. 'Daddy said you'd say that, too.'

Claudia backed away from the bed, struggling to keep her composure. 'How very clever Daddy was,' she said thickly, bitter tears stinging her eyes, making the room waver.

'Are you crying?' Natalie asked curiously.

Claudia raised a hand to brush away the telling moisture, and met the sympathetic gaze of the young woman across the bed. Colour flooded her cheeks. A stranger's pity was the last straw. She produced a cracked laugh.

'Don't be silly, Natalie, I'm sure Daddy told you I never cry!' she declared raggedly, drawing in a steadying breath as the words trembled. 'Well, I seem to be in the way, don't I? I'm sure you'd rather see Tyler on your own, so I'll wish you goodnight.' Her eyes flickered to Tyler and away again. 'I'll wait outside.' It was all she could manage. She had borne enough. With a hastily stifled sob she turned and hurried from the room.

In the corridor Claudia crossed to the nearest open window, gulping in fresh air desperately in an effort to stem the tears. They fell anyway, and she sagged helplessly against the wall. What Gordon had done was despicable. It hadn't been enough to have her believe Natalie was dead; he had had to alienate her from her daughter completely. So that, even if, as had happened, she should discover his lie, he had covered himself. He had left her with nothing.

'Mrs Peterson? Mrs Peterson, why don't you come and sit down?'

Lost in misery, Claudia hadn't realised she wasn't alone. She opened her eyes to find the young woman standing beside her, face creased into lines of concern. She was indicating a row of chairs near by. Claudia allowed herself to be led to one of them simply because she didn't have the will or the strength to argue. Shaking, she sank on to it and rested her head back against the wall, totally defeated.

'Is there anything I can get you, Mrs Peterson? Tea or coffee?'

Claudia's lips twisted into the travesty of a smile. 'Who are you?'

'I'm Wendy Nicholls, Mrs Peterson, Natalie's nanny. Well, more of a nurse and companion these days.'

'Oh, yes, I remember. Well, Miss Nicholls, the only thing I want nobody can get me,' she said dully.

Wendy sat down too. 'I'm sure Natalie didn't mean what she said.'

'Oh, yes, she did. Gordon made sure of that,' she contradicted bitterly. Turning her head, she looked at the other woman. 'Did you know my ex-husband?'

'Yes,' she said shortly, eyes on her hands.

Claudia stared at her, and slowly light dawned. 'I see,' she said slowly, meaningfully.

At that the nanny did look up. 'No, I don't think you do. I wasn't one of his . . . women,' she denied with distaste.

Blinking, Claudia sat up a little straighter. 'But he tried to make you one?' She caught the other woman's unease and smiled wryly. 'Oh, don't worry, you aren't going to shock me. I knew all about them.'

Wendy looked relieved. 'I wasn't sure. Some women . . . well, you know.'

'But they weren't married to Gordon. I knew because I was meant to know. He was unfaithful from the day we were married,' Claudia explained flatly, then looked at

Wendy curiously. 'I don't mean to be insulting, but I'd be interested to know why you refused. Usually they fell like ninepins for his charm and his handsome face.' Just as she herself had done.

'He was too handsome. Too smooth, too everything. I couldn't like him. Unlike Natalie. Your daughter is a very lovable little girl, Mrs Peterson. You didn't see the best of her today. She's shrewd. She loves Mr Monroe and me because she knows we love her. Unhappily, she knew, just as I did, that her father didn't really love her. It wasn't anything he said or did. To an outsider he was a doting father. It was just... instinct, I suppose.'

How Claudia envied her that insight. She could have done with just a pinch of it herself. As for the other, what Wendy had to say made her heart go out to her daughter. 'Oh, Natalie!'

Wendy Nicholls's face softened. 'It's not my place to make a judgement on why you left Natalie, Mrs Peterson, but I'd put all my savings on one thing: you do love her. So that's why I'm telling you not to give up because of what she said tonight. She needs your love, even if she doesn't know it. She hurt you because she doesn't know you or trust you. All she knows is what she's been told. You're going to have to overcome that. It won't be easy, I'm afraid, but if I'm right, and you do love her, you'll do it.'

Unsteadily Claudia's hand reached out to take the other woman's. 'Thank you. You don't know how much it means to me to hear you say that. I love Natalie very much. I always have. It warms my heart to know that, when I wasn't there, she had you to turn to. I only wish Tyler could understand as readily as you do. Does he have any idea that Natalie knows Gordon didn't love her?'

'I don't think so, Mrs Peterson. Sometimes the cleverest men don't see what's in front of their noses. Besides, your husband was awfully good at pulling the wool over people's eyes.'

'Except yours,' Claudia put in with a smile.

'Except mine,' Wendy agreed, returning the smile warmly, then glanced beyond Claudia's shoulder, making her turn.

Tyler strode towards them, face quite stern. 'Natalie's asking for you, Wendy. I've said goodnight, and told her I'll be back to see her before she goes down tomorrow,' he said, but his eyes were quartering Claudia's still pale face.

Wendy rose immediately. 'I'd better go, then. We'll see you tomorrow. Goodnight,

Mrs Peterson, it was nice to have met you.' She gave a general smile and hastened away, leaving Claudia and Tyler together.

They were silent for a moment, then Tyler cleared his throat. 'I'm sorry about Natalie's behaviour earlier.'

Claudia stood up smoothly and looked him squarely in the eye. 'Are you? Are you really? I thought you'd say it was all I deserved.'

A nerve ticked in his jaw. 'I knew she had no reason to welcome you, but I thought she had better manners. I had no idea she'd say what she did.'

'No,' Claudia agreed drily, 'I shouldn't imagine you would. But don't worry, there's no permanent harm done. She wanted to hurt me and she did. But I never imagined it was going to be a sinecure to get to know my daughter. Gordon never did make life easy.'

Tyler took her arm to guide her back to the lift. 'Gordon isn't to blame for Natalie's reaction. You did that all by yourself when you rejected her. Natalie's old enough to know when she's loved or not.'

The lift arrived and they stepped inside before Claudia answered.

'I hope so,' she declared fervently, 'because if there's one thing I can do for Natalie it's to make sure she knows just how very much I love her.'

He looked her over, brows raised. 'Very touching, Claudia. Then what will you do? Walk away again? You're trouble with a capital "T". I'm beginning to think I should never have brought you here.' The doors opened and Tyler stepped aside to allow her to walk out on to the ground floor, then swiftly led the way out to the car park.

Claudia hurried to keep up. 'I'm sorry to disappoint you, but you won't be getting rid of me that easily. I intend to stay, Tyler, and there's nothing you can do about it.'

He cast her a mocking look. 'You think not? Don't underestimate me.'

'Oh, I don't, but it's too late to have me fade back into the wallpaper.'

They had reached the car, but Tyler didn't immediately open the door. Instead he put out a hand and caught her chin.

'Perhaps it is, but you'd do well to remember that Gordon made me her guardian.'

Claudia's heart lurched, but she refused to back down. This was far too important. 'Is that a threat to stop me seeing her? You'd be laughed out of court—where you'll wind up if you try it! I'm her mother, and my rights are greater than yours, Tyler. Morally and legally.' She made a mental note to check that with her lawyer as soon as possible. 'No one has a greater right to see her than me!'

'Even if she doesn't want to see you?' he challenged, silky smooth and oh, so cutting.

She winced, pulling away as he drew first blood. 'Damn you!' She turned her back on him, lifting a hand to brush away weak tears. Pressing her lips tightly together, she swallowed hard. 'I know she hates me,' she whispered huskily, 'but I'd rather have that than nothing. I'm not too proud to admit I need her. I wouldn't hurt her, you must know that, but if you want my word, if you believe it means anything, then you have it. I won't do anything to upset her.'

In the silence that echoed her words all she could hear was her own ragged breathing. Then firm hands descended on her shoulders and turned her round. Insistent fingers raised her chin until their eyes met. His look was searching, appraising.

'Such humility. It's not how I remember you.'

Her lashes dropped. 'You don't know me— you never did,' she replied huskily.

'That, at least, we can agree on,' he taunted softly.

Something stirred in the air. 'Tyler —— '

'You should have stayed with Gordon,' he advised coldly, cutting her off.

He only succeeded in rousing her anger. 'How easy it is for you to say! Some sacrifices are just too harsh to contemplate. But you've never had to sacrifice anything, have you, Tyler? Let me tell you how it is. It hurts. It hurts so badly that you think you'll go mad. But you don't. You just have to live with the knowledge every second of every minute. Every hour of every day. For year after soul-destroying year! You've no idea how endless a minute can be when you're trying not to think! So, until you do know, don't you dare to preach to me about what I should or shouldn't have done!'

Even in the murky light she could see his nostrils flare as he took an angry breath. 'You're hysterical!'

'The typical male answer to everything! I'm not hysterical, but you're most definitely a self-satisfied, sanctimonious prig!'

'Name-calling will get you nowhere,' he re-joined tartly.

For no clear reason the words deflated her like a pricked balloon. 'Nothing has ever got me anywhere, neither playing by the rules nor ignoring them.'

'Feeling sorry for yourself isn't going to help either,' he said tersely, letting her go to bend and unlock the door.

Claudia stared at his downbent head. 'What will? Tell me and I'll do it. Anything, I swear,' she declared rashly, so close to the end of her tether that she was scarcely aware of what she meant or of how it would sound.

Not so Tyler; he straightened, face drawn into lines of distaste. 'That just about rounds off the day! Now get in the car before I'm tempted to give you a hiding that's been long overdue!'

Defeated and overwrought, Claudia could do little else than do as he said. All she was doing was making matters worse. Wearily she strapped herself in, and when he joined her she had to moisten a dry mouth in order to utter a simple, 'I'm sorry.'

To her surprise Tyler sighed heavily. 'Neither of us is acting very calmly. I suggest we go to the hotel, have something to eat, and relax. Then we'll talk, OK?' he said tiredly.

She didn't know if it would ever be possible for them to just talk, but it sounded good. 'All right.'

Without another word he started the engine, and the short journey was accomplished in silence. The hotel had been chosen for its nearness to the hospital, not its exclusivity, yet Tyler's suite was a haven of peace after a traumatic day. The décor was soothing and the couches deliciously inviting. However, as soon as he closed the door behind them Claudia felt the serenity begin to dissipate. She was alone with him now, truly alone for the first time in years, and her nervous system went into overdrive.

She watched as Tyler sank wearily into a comfortable-looking armchair, her breath lodging in her throat as he stretched, the action pulling jeans and shirt taut over his muscular frame.

'Do you want to eat here or downstairs?'

Tyler's question drew her eyes to him, and she flushed to realise he had been watching her watching him.

'I'm not really hungry.'

Tyler reached for the telephone. 'You can't go without food. You haven't eaten all day. I'll get them to send something up.'

She wasn't going to fight him. 'Please yourself, Tyler; you always do anyway. If you'll excuse me I want to have a shower and change.' Picking up her case, she glanced at the two doors in the far wall. 'Which room is mine?' She followed his inclination of the head and let out a thready sigh as she closed the door on him.

The relief was short-lived. There were two single beds in the room, and one of them showed clear signs of occupation. All her muscles stiffened in rejection. There was no way she could share a room with him.

When she opened the door again Tyler was just replacing the telephone. 'I'm afraid you're out of luck. There are no single rooms available here.' Catching her look of surprise, he shrugged. 'I anticipated your reaction— correctly, it seems. This is the height of the tourist season, and that means the hotel is filled to capacity.'

'There are other hotels,' she pointed out.

'True,' he conceded, 'but this is the nearest. I'm not running around all over town collecting you each day, Claudia. So, like it or not, that means you stay here.'

'And the other room?'

'Is a single, which Wendy uses. So, if you have no other questions, I suggest you go and have your shower. The food will be here in a few minutes.'

Damn him, he had an answer for everything! And she couldn't insist because the last thing she wanted to do was make him aware of just how vulnerable she truly was to his

closeness. She returned to the bedroom, re-
signing herself to having to share. If he could
contemplate it without turning a hair then she
would make sure she did the same. Even so,
unpacking her things into the wardrobe beside
Tyler's clothes had a familiar intimacy. It felt
right, and it made her think of what might
have been. Which was a pointless exercise.
Resolutely she closed the door, then took what
she needed into the bathroom.

She did feel better after her shower, a great
deal of the strain washing away with the soap.
She was just slipping into peach silk lounging
pyjamas when Tyler knocked on the door to
tell her the food had arrived. She still didn't
feel hungry, but she knew he was right—she
had to try to eat something.

A table had been laid by the window, and
Tyler was already there. Claudia was struck
by the intimacy of the setting. Once they had
shared many meals like this, meals that had
been full of love. Things impossible to forget
if she strove for a thousand years. Did it bring
back memories for him too? Or, she wondered bitterly, had he wiped her from his heart
and mind completely? His attitude surely said
he had, and suddenly she wished she'd found
something else to wear. The pyjamas, while
modest, hinted at the feminine curves be-

neath. She felt certain he would think she was attempting to lure him, which, of course, she wasn't. Seraphina had packed her clothes, knowing what she liked to wear for relaxing. It annoyed her to realise Tyler's behaviour actually had her on the verge of altering her habits. But why should she? She had nothing to be ashamed of. Having rallied her flagging spirit, she went to join him.

She had been expecting a heavy English meal, but was wrong. Tyler had ordered deliciously fluffy omelettes with salad. Instead of being repelled, her tastebuds sprang to life and she was soon tucking in with relish.

She threw him a curious look. 'I'm surprised you aren't using your flat. You told me once you lived in London.'

'I gave it up when I inherited a house in Shropshire four years ago. I found I could work just as effectively from there.'

With the first edge taken off her hunger, Claudia sat back, reaching for her untouched glass of wine and sipping it appreciatively. The fruity taste burst on her tongue and in her mind, triggering a flash of memories. Unsure, she sat up a little straighter and took another sip. The knowledge was confirmed, and she turned accusing eyes on Tyler as she set the glass down pointedly.

Sitting back in his chair, he returned her gaze limpidly. 'Something not to your taste? It's a California wine; one of the best.'

Claudia's hands curled into fists. 'And Gordon's favourite.'

Tyler smiled. 'I thought you'd appreciate the gesture.'

Somehow she held on to her temper. 'I would have thought you were above this sort of petty behaviour, Tyler.'

'I prefer to call it a timely reminder.'

Claudia ground her teeth together in frustration. He had no right to do this. 'Well, it was neither appreciated nor necessary. There's nothing about Gordon I'm ever likely to forget.'

'Unless it's convenient to do so. The further the distance, the shorter the memory. Is that why you chose to stay in Italy?' he queried cynically.

'You wouldn't be interested in why I live there, Tyler. It wouldn't fit into your scheme of things,' Claudia snapped back.

Tyler chose to ignore the remark, saying instead, 'That house—you were living there when we first met.'

She was surprised he cared to remember. 'That's right. It belongs to my aunt.'

His gaze quartered her. 'Did she know about us?' he demanded sharply.

'Oh, yes,' Claudia said steadily. 'You weren't a secret. I wasn't ashamed of knowing you. She approved,' she added, and thought she saw surprise cross his face. It was gone in an instant, though, leaving his expression distant.

'If I remember correctly you said she was an artist.'

'Still is,' Claudia agreed stiffly, a simmering anger coming to the boil again. 'I can see how your mind works, Tyler. You think she's Bohemian, with an odd idea of morality. That's not true. She doesn't believe women are men's chattels, bound to suffer in silence whatever their lord and master decrees. We have rights too, you know. We're entitled to happiness.'

'And the vows you made mean nothing?' he shot back derisively.

Claudia's eyes flashed. He knew nothing, and the unfairness of his charge hurt. 'Men take vows too, not just women. And break them.'

'I never said men were perfect,' Tyler countered predictably.

'But women should be, right?' she snapped with heavy irony. 'Like Caesar's wife, above suspicion?' Abruptly she rose to her feet and paced away, swinging round when she reached the couch. 'I'll tell you something that will really make you laugh. I was. Right up until the day I met you. My marriage was a farce, but I stood by my commitment. Even when I discovered what type of man I'd married, that he'd only married me for my money. Call it pride, but I never once abandoned those principles.'

Tyler turned in his seat. 'What you're saying is that only I persuaded you to break them?' he queried cynically. 'Supposing it were true, what made me so special?'

Claudia sank on to the arm of the couch, legs trembling. Did he think she would deny her feelings so easily? She had never taken the easy way out, and wasn't about to start now. 'You know the answer to that. I fell in love with you,' she admitted huskily. If she had expected to move him she was disappointed.

'And that gave you leave to lie to me? To pretend you were free?' he charged her coldly.

What was the point of telling him she was leaving Gordon? Had already left him in spirit, if not in fact? She chose to return the ball to his court. 'Until you told me about your mother I had no reason to expect you wouldn't understand,' she countered.

'Whereupon you promptly fell out of love with me and ran back to Gordon. How touching!' he scoffed.

Claudia gasped in disbelief. 'I went back to England because you gave me no choice,' she protested. 'If you remember, you walked out on me.'

Tyler's lips curved without humour. 'You'd have me feel sympathy for you, yet it couldn't have been that bad. Apparently you didn't dislike your marriage enough to deny Gordon your bed,' he declared caustically. 'So let's have the truth now, Claudia. Did you ever really love me?'

So much that I would have willingly died for you, her heart cried. Pride, however, dictated her answer. She shrugged, and said aloud, 'Isn't that beside the point now?'

'I was just your holiday fling?' he queried tersely.

Even her pride couldn't let that pass. 'You were never that, Tyler,' she denied hoarsely.

'Wasn't I?' he challenged, standing and coming across to her. 'When I saw you at the anniversary do I knew why you'd lied to me. My own cousin's wife, and I never realised! You really played me for a fool, didn't you?'

Claudia shook her head helplessly. 'I never did that, Tyler, though I don't expect you to believe me. I had no idea you and Gordon were related. I never expected to see you again.'

'Hoped you wouldn't,' he shot back swiftly. 'You looked horrified when you saw me. No doubt you thought I was going to give your game away.'

With first-hand knowledge of his feelings she had fully expected him to. 'Why didn't you tell him?'

Tyler snorted in self-disgust. 'God knows! It's what I should have done.'

'I thank you for it, anyway.'

The chilly remoteness was back in a flash. 'Don't thank me. I didn't do it for you. I found nothing noble in telling Gordon how unfaithful his wife was when it meant admitting I was the guilty party.'

As if she had just been slapped in the face Claudia winced. 'If that was how it felt to you then your love was a very shallow thing, Tyler. Perhaps it's just as well it's all water under the bridge now,' she said sadly, feeling more betrayed now than at the time.

Tyler tipped his head forward. 'You aren't going to try and justify yourself? Most women would.'

She looked up at him furiously. 'I'm not most women. I'm me, and I don't have to

justify myself to anyone. But, if you're interested enough to hear my side of the story, I'll
tell you.'

He smiled broadly at that and dropped into
the nearest armchair, crossing his legs comfortably. 'I'm past the age for fairy-stories,
Claudia. Your record is all down in black and
white in the newspaper archives. If I ever want
to read it I know where to go.'

Claudia gave up. She was getting nowhere,
just battering herself against an indomitable
brick wall. Sighing, she swung her legs round
and sank into the corner of the couch.

'Do you always believe what you read in
the newspapers?' she asked, not masking her
own contempt.

Resting his elbow on the arm, Tyler supported his chin on his fingers. 'Isn't it true?'

His smugness was a red rag. 'Actually the
papers were quite accurate for once. I did
everything they said.' Only they never asked
her why she did the things she did, and neither
did Tyler now.

The look he gave her was chilling, but she
was getting used to that. 'It's hardly something to be proud of. If you intend to spend
any time at all with Natalie I suggest you curb
your penchant for wildness. I don't think it
would amuse her, or help your cause, to see

your name plastered all over the front pages of the gutter Press.'

Claudia glanced down at her hands for a moment while she controlled her temper, then she met his gaze squarely. 'That isn't likely to happen, and if you stopped to think for a minute you'd know it. I'm as concerned about Natalie as you are. I know my sudden reappearance in her life isn't going to be easy for either of us, but I don't intend to force myself on her. I want my daughter, but I want her willingly.'

Tyler returned her gaze soberly. 'And if she isn't willing?'

'I'll face that when...if...the time comes,' Claudia said quietly.

Tyler continued to watch her thoughtfully, but whatever decision he came to he kept to himself. Finally he glanced at his watch. 'It's late—we'd better get some sleep. You can use the bathroom first.'

She sighed, then hastily stifled a yawn. 'Thanks, I will.' She climbed wearily to her feet. 'Goodnight.'

She went into the bedroom, closing the door softly behind her. She felt drained, totally spent. Wearily she took her night things from the dresser and carried them into the bathroom to change. She wasn't taking any chances of having Tyler walk in on her.

In the event, he didn't come into the bedroom until she had been in bed some time. Lying on her side, through her lashes she watched as his fingers began to deal with his shirt buttons. They were beautiful hands, not workmanlike or even practical, simply beautiful. Long-fingered, artistic. She remembered the tenderness of them so well.

Out of the blue, stinging tears burnt the backs of her eyes and she squeezed them tight. It was not the time to remember such things. It never would be. When Tyler walked silently past her and into the bathroom she buried her head in her pillow as the silent tears ran free. How she wished she could forget, but knew it was impossible. Some things were just meant to be that way.

Closing her eyes, she willed sleep to come quickly.

CHAPTER FOUR

CLAUDIA didn't remember falling asleep, but she woke next morning to the sound of the shower running. For a moment she was completely disorientated, unable to recall where she was or why. Then memory returned—Tyler, the flight, Natalie—and she struggled upright. Tyler chose that particular moment to come back into the room, hair shiny with moisture, chest and feet bare, and wearing jeans that were moulded to his body.

Though he took no notice of her as he reached into the wardrobe for a clean shirt, Claudia couldn't stop her eyes from following him. There wasn't an ounce of spare flesh on his very masculine body, and she felt her blood begin to pump thick and heavy through her veins. The wanting was still there, burning as hot and fierce as ever it had done in those heady days so long ago. But stronger still was the need to be held with love, to be given comfort and a safe harbour—things he wouldn't give her. Because of them, passion could never be enough.

Tyler fastened the last button and began rolling up the sleeves of his shirt. Her eyes traced the movement automatically, then rose higher. Her nerves gave a violent jolt as she found herself looking into a pair of sardonic blue eyes. To her chagrin she realised he had been fully aware of her inspection.

'Hungry?' he asked her, an eyebrow lifting interrogatively.

Claudia's eyes widened. 'What?'

Sitting on the end of his bed, he quickly put on socks and shoes, before glancing over his shoulder. 'Do you want breakfast?'

He hadn't meant that at all, and they both knew it. It was ridiculous to feel hurt by the cheap implication, but she was. He had that power, and always would. All the same, she masked it with a sweep of her hand through her hair that, she noted with acid amusement, drew his eyes to the generous swell of her breasts, barely covered by silk and lace.

'Just coffee will do.'

Blue eyes met brown and glittered with icy amusement. 'Sure I can't interest you in anything else?' he provoked further.

Meeting the challenge, Claudia produced an acid smile. 'Thanks, but I'm not that hungry.'

He stood up, hands resting negligently on his hips. 'Palate jaded, is it? That often happens with over-indulgence.'

Her eyes flashed in a totally Latin reaction. 'I take it you speak from experience. I remember you had quite an appetite yourself!'

Tyler's smile was wolfish. 'True, but then something rotten spoiled it, and it never returned.'

Wincing inwardly at her stupidity in allowing herself to be drawn into the exchange, Claudia drew up her knees and wrapped her arms around them. 'Trading insults on an empty stomach was never my ideal start of the day, but it's no novelty to me. So, if it pleases you, carry on. You won't draw blood.'

He appeared genuinely amused this time. 'You think that's what I'm after?'

She looked at him steadily. 'Aren't you? You're Gordon's cousin, even if the connection is remote. Nothing would surprise me.'

His grin faded. 'You make it sound as if he was some sort of devil.'

'He was diabolically clever at discovering a person's weak spot and using it against them. Perhaps you should think about that, Tyler, because nobody escaped him. He did it to you, only you refuse to accept it.'

'Perhaps because the Gordon you describe doesn't match the man I knew.'

Claudia sighed. '*Nobody* knew him, don't you see? Gordon was a chameleon.'

Tyler smiled. 'He certainly knew how to make himself acceptable to people.'

'Precisely. How else would he get his own way? He was so good at it. But answer me this: would you consider Gordon a secure financial risk?'

Tyler started to speak, then stopped, eyes narrowing. 'Very clever.'

Claudia shrugged. She'd started him thinking, at least, testing his integrity in his own field. At work he judged people unemotionally, and she wanted him to do that with Gordon. Now she backed off. 'What time is the operation?'

'Ten o'clock. You'd better get a move on,' Tyler directed shortly, clearly annoyed by her remarks. He went out, and seconds later she heard him talking on the telephone.

Climbing from the bed, Claudia gathered fresh clothes and hastened into the bathroom. It was steamy still and carried the scent of Tyler's aftershave. She had to harden herself against the tug it wielded on her senses. The lightweight cream two-piece she had picked up was elegant yet cool, and gave her a touch-me-not air. Pretty flimsy armour against the two people she loved and who seemed determined to hurt her if they could.

Although, she thought as she used make-up sparingly to emphasise her eyes, there was nothing unusual in that. Tyler was probably a hopeless case, but Natalie was different. She must keep Wendy Nicholls' words in mind, because they offered her her only real hope of success.

Not that that seemed to help as she approached Natalie's room beside Tyler an hour later. They had made a brief detour, at her request, to a famous toyshop, where Claudia had agonised over the purchase of a doll, finally deciding on one that the assistant informed her was the most popular. The trouble was that she had no idea if Natalie was a tomboy or not. Tyler had said nothing, and it was clear that he had decided she must make her own mistakes with her daughter.

Her heart quailed as she followed Tyler into the room. What would her daughter's reaction be today? She wasn't long in finding out. Of the two people in the room only Wendy had a smile for her. Natalie's attention was fixed rigidly on Tyler. Having already had her pre-op injection, she was a little woozy, yet she produced a wobbly smile and held out her arms.

'Tyler!' Her delight and relief were unfeigned, but as she tightened her arms about Tyler's neck her eyes found her mother and issued a message that Claudia had no trouble interpreting: See, you aren't wanted, so why don't you go away?

Just as firmly her eyes told the little girl that she was staying anyway.

Almost flouncing, Natalie released Tyler and sank back against her pillows. 'Why did you bring *her* here?' she demanded petulantly.

'She has a right to be here, scamp,' Tyler explained gently.

Rebellious eyes glared at her mother. 'Nobody asked you to come!'

Claudia, recognising hurt beneath that cruel truth, took a steadying breath. 'No, nobody did. I came because I wanted to. That's what mothers do.' Given the chance.

'You didn't come when I had measles, or when I broke my arm,' Natalie was swift to point out.

'I would have done if I'd known, believe me.'

'I don't believe you,' Natalie cried, and turned to the man beside her. 'Make her go away, Tyler,' she pleaded tearfully.

Tyler took her in his arms and soothed her, and Claudia was torn by an unexpected wave of jealousy. She wanted to be the one Natalie turned to. Then immediately despised herself for the emotion. Of course Natalie wanted Tyler, for she had grown up with him. It was her mother who was the outsider.

But I didn't want to be, her heart cried as she turned away to stare out of the window. Her eyes burnt with unshed tears—a mixture of anger and self-pity. Both emotions were pointless and destructive, and she shook her head, dismissing them.

She could hear Tyler's voice, murmuring low words of comfort and encouragement, and Natalie's answering, though what she said she couldn't make out. She realised that setting herself apart here because she was hurting too, was wrong. However painful rejection was, she had to battle against it, pretend she had a thick skin, and hope, one day, to win Natalie's confidence.

With a soft sigh she returned to the bed and stood looking down at her now subdued daughter. 'I'm sorry you feel this way, Natalie. I didn't mean to upset you. One day you'll understand that things can't always be the way we want them.' There was little point in saying more to a pair of unreceptive ears, so instead she took the lid from the box she held and placed it across her daughter's knees. 'I've brought you something I thought might cheer you up,' she said with a hopeful smile.

Wendy, who had been a silent observer of the exchange, leant over to see the present. 'Oh, what a lovely doll. Say "thank you", Natalie,' she prompted.

'Thanks,' the word came grudgingly.

Claudia felt totally helpless. 'If you don't like it I can always change it for something else,' she offered.

'Did Tyler tell you I wanted one?' the young girl demanded suspiciously.

Recalling his silence on the subject, Claudia smiled wryly. 'No, it was all my own idea. Is it all right?'

Natalie shrugged, 'It's OK, I guess.'

Damned with faint praise, Claudia was searching for an answer to that when they came to take Natalie down to the theatre. It was awful to see her being wheeled away, looking so small and fragile. Even Wendy's bracing smile as she accompanied her charge couldn't dispel Claudia's throat-clenching anxiety. The silence that descended on the room once Natalie had gone stretched her nerves, and, swallowing a lump in her throat, she turned to Tyler. The cheerfulness he had assumed for Natalie's benefit faded now, and he looked pale and tense as he ran a hand around his neck and took a deep breath.

'You can go now if you want to,' he told her, shocking her to the core.

'What?' Claudia gasped, unable to believe he'd actually said it.

Tyler glared at her irritably. 'There's no point in your hanging around here. They'll be hours yet. Natalie won't know if you were here or not. You could get in some shopping.'

It hurt that he could callously believe she would just leave, but it was so typical of his attitude towards her she wondered why she was continually surprised. 'All the same, I'm staying.'

'Trying to earn some Brownie points?' he enquired mockingly, then shrugged and turned away. 'Please yourself.'

They were the last words he addressed to her for over an hour. He stood by the window, hands stuffed into his pockets, looking out, but she could see by the tension in his back and shoulders that he saw nothing. Claudia sat down on one of the chairs, her eyes scarcely leaving him. How she wished she could go to him and hold him. To give and receive comfort and reassurance.

Suddenly she could bear the silence and the distance no longer. It was ridiculous. They should be helping not ignoring each other. 'She'll be all right, Tyler, you'll see,' she encouraged softly.

His head jerked round. 'That's your informed opinion, is it?' he jeered, and, unable to hide her hurt at the injustice of that remark, Claudia got to her feet quickly and swept up her bag from the bed.

'I'm going to get myself a cup of coffee—do you want some?' she asked huskily, head averted. She heard a sharp sigh.

'Damn! I'm sorry. There was no call for that. I realise you're just as worried,' he apologised.

She let out a shaky breath. 'Thank you.'

'I shouldn't take out my mood on you.'

Claudia smiled wryly. 'I've broad shoulders. Why don't you talk to me? It will help, I know. Tell me about Natalie, Tyler.'

'I'll get us that coffee. It's going to be a long morning.'

He was right—it dragged by with nerve-stretching slowness, but through it he talked. That he cared deeply was obvious, and Claudia listened intently, trying to fill the gap of time.

It seemed a whole lifetime had passed before footsteps could be heard approaching the door, and, unlike all the others, this time didn't go right on by. They both looked round expectantly, and Claudia stood up. The white-coated doctor who entered nodded to Claudia and smiled at Tyler.

'You can relax now, Mr. Monroe. The operation was a complete success. Natalie is in the recovery-room at the moment, but we'll be bringing her back here very shortly.'

Pure relief from the appalling tension made Claudia's head spin. 'Thank God!' Tears blurred her vision as she looked at Tyler, but she saw the glint of moisture in his own eyes. Unnoticed, the doctor slipped away, leaving them facing each other.

What she did next was instinctive and un-planned. Half laughing, half crying, she went to him, and, wonder of wonders, Tyler opened his arms to her, sweeping her in to a bone-crushing embrace. Claudia didn't care, but clung to him as he buried his face against her neck. Comfort was what they both needed, and she gave it willingly, hands gently stroking the taut planes of his back.

'Didn't I tell you?' she gasped joyfully, dis-tributing tiny kisses in an excess of relief.

A reluctant laugh broke from him. He raised his head, and as he did so her lips came into sudden and shocking contact with his. They both froze. But only for a moment, for with a groan Tyler brought his head down, and his lips took hers in a kiss that brooked no opposition.

Claudia had no thought of denying him. Her lips opened beneath his assault like petals in sunlight and welcomed his exploration of her mouth, returning his kiss feverishly. For mindless seconds they were oblivious to the world about them. Claudia arched her neck in delight as Tyler's lips left hers and set out on a heated exploration of the sensitive flesh of her throat. Shivers of exquisite pleasure danced across her skin as his avid mouth searched even lower, only to be stopped by the barrier of her clothes.

Once more he groaned, but it was as if that brought him to his senses, for his hands bit into her flesh as he abruptly thrust himself away from her. Face contorted with an emotion Claudia couldn't name, he shook his head as if to clear it of a thick fog.

'Dear God! I must be out of my mind!' he declared hoarsely, expression now one of utter disgust.

Claudia drew in a pained breath as something beautiful inside her died. To be in his arms had been to come home—a sanctuary he now denied her again. There was an instant when she wanted to scream out her agony of heart, but she controlled it with an effort that made her whole body shake. She turned her back on him, disguising the move by swiftly gathering up her bag and reaching inside it for her compact. Powdering an imaginary shine on her nose with a hand that wasn't quite steady, she responded, 'That makes two of us. That wasn't what I came here for.' Somehow the words came out cool and steady. Enough, anyway, to fool Tyler, and that was what she wanted.

'Wasn't it?' he challenged. 'Just what exactly are you after, Claudia?'

Face composed once more, she snapped the compact shut and swung round. 'Natalie. That's all. That kiss was a mistake. We were both over-emotional. Believe me, it won't happen again.'

'You're damn right it won't!' Tyler returned savagely. 'In future stay well away from mė.'

If it were any other man she would have accused him of protesting too much, but this was Tyler. 'It will be my pleasure,' she agreed with a blithe smile that hid a great deal. What had been a glorious reawakening for her had been nothing special to him. It debased her feelings, crumbling away the edges of fond memories. She could almost hate him for that, because they were all she had left of him.

An uneasy silence fell and it was an infinite relief when Natalie was finally wheeled back into the room. Claudia's heart constricted at the sight of her daughter, looking so small and vulnerable as she lay hooked up to vital monitors.

Her first attempt to speak was a mere croak and she hastily cleared her blocked throat. 'How long will Natalie have to remain in hospital?'

Tyler came to the foot of the bed. 'Hopefully not too long. Although it was heart surgery, I imagine it could be classed as routine these days.'

'But she'll be able to live a normal life now?' Claudia pursued, needing reassurance.

'Oh, yes.'

Claudia trailed her fingers over the coverlet. She didn't suppose she'd be truly convinced until she saw it for herself. 'When I was carrying I didn't care if my baby was a boy or a girl. All I wanted was for it to be healthy. I never realised what she must have suffered. I should have been there!'

'You should also have been there when she took her first steps, and when she formed her first real words. You should have been there to see the pictures she painted at the play-group and brought home so proudly. And let's not forget the time she was Mary in the Sunday school nativity play!' Tyler enlarged with all the precision of a master torturer.

Claudia listened in silent horror, each intake of breath an agony as he drove home his barbs. He was doing it on purpose, she knew, trying to break her—and he succeeded. 'For God's sake!' The cry broke through white lips. She turned away from him, going to the window and hanging on grimly to the sill. Tyler followed. She sensed him standing behind her, like Nemesis waiting to pounce. 'I would have crawled on my knees to be with her for all those things, if only I'd known she was alive! But, as God is my witness, I didn't know!' she declared, looking round.

He was pale too. 'So you're still sticking to that story, are you?'

'Why would I lie?' she cried angrily.

'Women seem to find it easy,' Tyler condemned.

Claudia turned fully to face him. 'Are we talking about me or your mother?' She used the only weapon she had.

His face closed up in distaste. 'Leave her out of this.'

'That's not possible, and you know it. She's at the centre of everything.'

'I said drop it, Claudia!' he warned in a voice that could crack rocks. 'Or, so help me, I'll . . .'

She refused to back off. 'Or what? You'll what? Hit me? Is that what your father did to your mother to drive her away?'

The fury in him was awesome, all the more so when he spoke in such a controlled voice. 'For your information, he begged her to stay with him.'

'That wasn't what I asked,' Claudia countered.

'No, he did not hit her.' The words were spaced out like bullets. 'Does that satisfy your disgusting curiosity?'

Not by a long way. She forgot her own hurt, intrigued by his past that had served to wreck their future. 'Then there was some other reason. Didn't she ever try to contact you?'

'I never received a single letter,' Tyler informed her curtly. 'Nor were any of mine answered.'

Twenty years on, Claudia could have wept for him. 'Oh, Tyler!'

'Don't waste your pity. It taught me a valuable lesson—not to put my faith in women. And I was right, as you proved to me.'

'And your father? What did he do?'

Blue eyes became flinty. 'Do, my dear Claudia? He drank himself to death within a year. That's what he did. That's what she did to him! Not a very pleasant story, is it?'

Her throat contracted, but she knew better than to offer him the sympathy she felt. 'But what happened to you?'

There was a softening in him, a relaxing of tensed muscles. 'I went to live with my grandparents, and I was very happy there. End of story. End of inquisition. Now you know every sordid detail. I've satisfied your curiosity and I don't want to hear another word about it,' he ordered and walked away to sit down beside Natalie.

Claudia's eyes followed him. No wonder he was bitter. He had been badly hurt when he was too young to understand. It was easy to see how the boy had become the man who still believed his mother had betrayed him and been responsible for his father's tragic death. Perhaps it was true. Perhaps it had all happened the way he'd said, but something inside her just didn't think so. Something that convinced her there was more to the story than that.

The compulsion to find his mother grew. She was the key to everything. The only person capable of making him rethink the past. Beyond that she didn't dare think. To consider what such a meeting might mean to them was going too far. Because, quite frankly, she didn't believe there was a 'them' any more, nor ever likely to be. Too much had happened. They could never go back and recapture the past, and every time he hurt her she didn't even know if she really wanted to. If only she didn't still love him so much.

Changing position for the nth time, Claudia stifled a sigh and carefully reached for the watch that lay on the bedside table. Turning the dial to catch what meagre light there was, she discovered it was just after one o'clock in the morning. With a silent groan she sank back on to her pillows. She'd been tossing and turning for hours, and she knew she was still too keyed up to sleep.

They had spent hours at Natalie's bedside waiting for her to come round. It had been a monumental relief when she had, but she hadn't stayed awake for long. Whereupon they had taken the sister's advice to go home and get some sleep themselves. Conversation over dinner had been stilted, to put it mildly, and after Tyler had placed a last call to the hospital to check that all was still well Claudia had been thankful to escape into the relative privacy of the bedroom.

She had been pretending to sleep when Tyler had eventually come to bed, but she knew from the sound of his breathing that he was soundly in the arms of Morpheus. It only served to make her feel more restive, because it pointedly reminded her how far apart they were.

She felt under an intense emotional strain. Two days of pretending she didn't care that she was being rejected, and she was already beginning to fray. She cared very much, and always would, because she couldn't love either of them moderately. What she felt was immoderate—all-encompassing. So that it was a kind of torture not to be able to show it. She had so much love to give, but neither wanted it, for their own different reasons. Tyler considered it base coin, and Natalie... Cruelly her daughter had been brought up to believe her mother didn't love her, while knowing her father didn't either.

How she longed to be able to right that wrong. She had known the emptiness of loneliness, when those you loved were lost to you, but had never expected Natalie to have suffered that too. She had to thank God for Tyler and Wendy Nicholls giving her a stable life, full of obvious affection. Yet it was only natural to feel jealous, to want to be able to give her own affection, which was her right.

The need was a pain inside that brought her upright. There was only one way she could ease it, and the hotel was the wrong place. She needed to be with Natalie. Just to sit with her would help, and perhaps, in some mysterious way, Natalie might feel a little of the love that was hers.

The thought was father to the deed. Climbing from the bed, quietly so as to avoid disturbing Tyler, Claudia searched quickly for her clothes, finally slipping into the bathroom to don jeans and sweater. Shoes and bag she collected on her way out past the still figure of Tyler. She tidied her hair in the lift on the way down, and only breathed a sigh of relief when she was in a taxi on her way back to the hospital.

It was rather eerie walking the empty corridors at night, but nobody questioned her right to be there. A low light glowed in

Natalie's room as Claudia pushed the door open. Wendy Nicholls was using it to read by. As Claudia stopped in surprise the young nanny glanced up, smiled when she saw who it was, and rose quickly, a finger to her lips.

'Have you come to sit with Natalie?' she asked in an undertone.

Claudia's fingers tightened on her bag. 'If it will be all right. I couldn't sleep, you see, and...' She tailed off, glancing revealingly beyond Wendy's shoulder to where her daughter lay.

'Of course it's all right. And I do understand,' Wendy said with ready sympathy. 'Take my chair. I'll leave you alone for a while. If you *should* need help there's a buzzer by the bed.' Smiling, she slipped quietly from the room.

Left alone with her daughter, Claudia approached the bed. Natalie was soundly asleep, face delicately flushed amid a halo of hair. Her heart swelled. She had been right to come. Peace surrounded her at once as she drew the chair nearer to the sleeping child, bringing a soothing balm to her soul.

'Oh, Natalie,' Claudia's voice was barely audible, 'you can't know how much I missed you, and how very much I love you. I want to be a real mother to you, to make things right. You're so perfect. Everything a mother could want in a daughter.' Tenderly she reached out to brush a strand of hair from one downy cheek. 'He told us both such monstrous lies that I don't know if I can ever overcome them. What am I going to do if you keep turning away? I thought that life had nothing for me, but now there's you. I have such plans for us—you can't imagine! Please...give me a chance to prove I care, darling. I won't let you down, I swear.'

The child made no movement, but Claudia hadn't expected her to. She sat back with a sigh of near-contentment. She didn't sleep, but she didn't think either. Her mind was blessedly free of anything but a new tranquillity.

Wendy came back, but, apart from sharing a smile of understanding, she didn't urge Claudia to go home. She only left when it grew light and sounds of activity began to echo along the corridors.

Rising a little stiffly to her feet, she gave her daughter one last look before turning to the young nanny. 'I'll go now, before she stirs. I don't want to take the risk of upsetting her. Thanks for letting me stay,' she said in a low tone.

'No one has a greater right to be here, Mrs Peterson,' Wendy insisted.

Claudia's smile was wry. 'I'm afraid others don't see it that way.' She hesitated a moment before adding, 'It's an imposition, I know, but I'd rather like to keep this secret for a while.'

'I think that could be arranged,' Wendy agreed, and watched thoughtfully as the young woman with the tragic eyes left.

Outside in the street, Claudia glanced around for a taxi, but there was none in sight. She walked to the end of the road and tried again. There was one, but its flag was down, and she was just about to set off for the nearest tube when, much to her surprise, a black Porsche did a U-turn and growled to a halt beside her.

'*Cara*, you look awful. Get in and I'll give you a lift,' a sexily accented voice declared from inside.

'Marco?' Claudia couldn't believe her ears, but, bending down to glance inside, she recognised the grinning face of her cousin. She climbed in, returning his friendly kiss. 'What are you doing here?' The last time she had seen him was at a rather wild party in Milan some months ago.

As he drove her to the hotel he explained he was in London on holiday. He had been to a party the previous evening and had only seen her by accident on his way home. Knowing something of his personal life, Claudia didn't reprove him, though it saddened her to see the pain still in his eyes. Instead she told him about Natalie, warmed by his ready concern.

Outside her hotel, he climbed out to help her alight with all the gallantry of his Latin nature. It made her laugh. His invitation to have dinner with him if she ever needed a friendly ear she accepted gratefully. They kissed again, and then she waved him off.

Still with a hint of a smile on her lips she turned to the entrance and encountered a chilling blue gaze. The smile faded abruptly. Her heart shot into her throat as she saw the icy contempt on Tyler's face, then it sank like lead to her stomach. She knew exactly what he was thinking, and how incriminating the scene he had undoubtedly witnessed looked.

He said nothing, though—he didn't need to—as he escorted her to the lift. He waited until they were safely inside the suite before unleashing the biting lash of his tongue.

'So, you couldn't wait!' he accused in a voice laced with disgust.

Claudia dropped her bag on to a chair and swung round to face him, in no mood to mince her words either. 'No, I couldn't,' she agreed, her chin raised defiantly, brown eyes flashing a warning he ignored.

Unaware that she wasn't confirming his accusation but her own actions, Tyler's face became stony and a nerve began to tick in his jaw. 'You were warned, Claudia.'

'Don't threaten me when you have no proof,' she countered swiftly.

'Proof!' he exploded. 'I awake to discover you're missing, and when I get down to the lobby it's to witness that tender lovers' farewell! What more proof do I need?'

Dear lord, he made her so angry! 'Why don't you ask me where I've been, what I've been doing?' she invited cuttingly.

He advanced on her then, to take her shoulders in a grip that made her gasp. 'I don't need words to know what's been going on.'

Her eyes narrowed, cat-like. 'Because you remember it all so clearly? Were you jealous, Tyler?' she challenged rashly and knew, with a wild elation, that she had pushed him too far.

A savage look came into his eyes that froze her heart. 'Jealous of other men's leavings?

Oh, no, sweetheart, this is what I think of that!' he declared and brought his mouth down crushingly on hers.

It hurt as it was meant to do, the tender skin tearing against her teeth until she tasted her own blood. Long-suppressed emotions surfaced, and she fought him, using her fists against his back until he was forced to grab for her wrists, capturing them too easily, without even lifting his lips from hers. He forced her arms down behind her and in so doing brought her body hard against his.

She gasped at the shock of that vital contact, aware of every solidly muscled inch of him. Yet it only spurred her on to an even greater frenzy, using her knees and feet, the sole weapons he had left her with. It worked to an extent, for he was forced to relinquish her lips as a kick went home, but only long enough to swear under his breath and thrust a leg between hers, jerking her feet out from under her.

With a cry of alarm, Claudia felt herself falling backwards. She had forgotten all about the couch, and it was just as much of a shock to have that break her fall as to have Tyler fall with her. For a few vital seconds the breath was knocked out of her. Not so Tyler. He took full advantage of her momentary immobility to anchor her down with the full weight of his body.

She opened her eyes in time to see his head lowering, to witness the grim determination on his face an instant before his mouth descended on hers, demanding submission. Claudia denied him with lips pressed tightly closed, appallingly aware of a fountainhead of warmth growing inside her. She knew it for what it was—desire, hot and heady. In dismay she realised that she had forgotten quite how it felt to have Tyler this close to her, even in anger. Senses that had lain dormant leapt into active life—shocking in their depth and violence.

Unable to move as his assault went on, she willed herself not to betray what she was feeling—prayed for the strength to continue denying him, though she craved to respond. For to do so in the face of his anger and contempt would be crushing. He mustn't know, must never be allowed to guess, for then what vengeance could he take!

If only he would stop! Dear God, he *must* stop now, before… From a distance she heard Tyler groan, and his lips stilled on hers. Then he was releasing her hands, coming up on his elbows to stare down into hectic eyes, face flushed and contorted with anger—and something else. Something her startled senses recognised and took her breath away. Yes, he was angry, but he wanted her. It was there, a stark message he took no trouble to hide.

Despite herself, she felt that sweet flood of desire spread throughout her body with a bone-melting weakness that set her heart thudding madly. Though every instinct urged her to move, she couldn't. Could only stare back as his eyes dropped to her now trembling lips.

His words were a muttered croak. 'Damn you, Claudia. Damn you,' he declared as, compelled, his head descended once more.

It was her undoing. With a shivering gasp, her lips parted helplessly to the command of his, and with a growl of victory Tyler took the advantage, his tongue sliding possessively into the warm depths of her mouth. All sense of precaution, of self-preservation was swept away on a pulsing wave of sensation. With an incoherent moan she returned his kiss, her tongue flicking out to join with his in a sensual exploration so intimately erotic that her mind could register nothing but the glory of it as the intervening years rolled away.

She could hold nothing back as her hands came up about his waist, fingers clutching feverishly at the fabric of his shirt. The reasons for her lying so close within his arms were forgotten as their lips locked in passionate imitation of the closeness their bodies craved. Her world shrank to the reality of his hard length upon her boneless body, hearing only Tyler's ragged breathing as his body moved restlessly on hers.

The empty ache inside her that she had managed to ignore these last years now clamoured for appeasement. She wanted... Coherent thought took wing as Tyler's hand insinuated its way beneath her sweater, gliding over the skin of her ribs to close about her breast. With a gasping sigh of pleasure she tore her lips from his, feeling herself swell into the cup of his hand. Her eyes opened, but she saw nothing, only felt the moist breath as Tyler's lips traced kisses over her cheek and jaw, and the steady rubbing of his thumb over her aching nipple that sent wave after wave of heat to the very core of her.

His body heat scorched her as he moved impatiently, pushing her sweater away to substitute warm lips for his teasing thumb. Back and forth the open lips traced their havoc-wreaking path, before closing hotly on the jutting peak.

'Tyler!' His name was a husky groan as Claudia drowned in the pleasure this suckling created.

Instinct took over for her as Tyler's love-making followed the well-remembered path. The hot pressure of his lips travelled the contours of her breasts to the twin peak, subjecting it to the same sensual torture. Small moans of delight forced their way from her throat, mingling with his own sounds of pleasure. Lost in an erotic world of passion, Tyler slid between her thighs, his hands slipping down to grasp her hips and hold her firmly to him. He moved against her in mute parody as his lips plundered her neck, kissing the sensitive skin hotly.

'Dear God, you taste so good. Feel how I want you.'

She could, and the sense of power in knowing she could make him feel like this was heady. With a whimper of need she entangled her hands in his hair to draw his head up to hers. 'Yes, darling. Oh, yes...yes.'

Her words were an echo of his, but they triggered off a reaction those previously heated moments hadn't prepared her for. Tyler went still in her arms, and the tension in him seemed to fill the air about them. She froze too, as the passion died away, yet his head came up as if at her bidding. Only it was dislike that was revealed to her in the deep blue of his eyes, shrivelling her up inside.

'No!' With that strangled cry of rejection Tyler tore himself out of her arms, to land on his knees beside the couch, breathing deeply.

Shivering in the shock of his abrupt withdrawal, Claudia struggled to sit up and right her clothes. Her body ached from the sudden denial, but that only served to remind her that they had been perilously close to the point of no return. A consummation her senses craved for, but which her mind and heart knew could only lead to even greater unhappiness.

They were two highly volatile substances that, put together, proved combustible. It had always been so, and now they had unwittingly proved that it still was so. But there was no future in it, no rebirth from the ashes—only a white-hot destruction. A brief moment of unequalled glory, followed by a lifetime of despair. Because for Tyler nothing had changed, nor ever would.

As he proved now by throwing her a look of crushing distaste. 'God, I knew that bringing you here was a mistake! I should never have let you back into my life,' he added as he dragged a hand through his hair.

Claudia flinched inwardly, a bitter twist to her lips. 'Don't worry, you haven't. I know my place. I know that wanting me sickens you. Well, I don't feel proud of myself, either,' she said thickly and gasped as his hand on her chin jerked her head round.

Blue eyes pierced hers. 'Knowing who you are, what you've done, why the hell do I still want you?' he demanded hoarsely.

His rigid beliefs hammered at her. 'You should ask yourself that, not me.'

His look darkened. 'Perhaps I should take you anyway. Get you out of my system once and for all.'

Claudia felt her anger surge at his arrogance. 'But it might not work that way, Tyler. You might find yourself addicted instead!' she taunted, pulling free of his hold.

His anger was tangible, seething between them. 'Don't you think I know that? Yet you tempt me. You're a fever in my blood. I look at you, and I want to drown in your passion.' His words, for all their vehemence, stirred her blood afresh, restricting her breathing as he went on. 'But, as God is my witness, I'll fight this need. I'll cure myself of you one way or another.'

A dull pain wrung her heart. 'And if you don't?' she questioned huskily.

Tyler rose to his feet, once more in complete control of his emotions. 'I will, because there will never be a place for you in my life. The only bond between us is Natalie. I intend to keep it that way.'

He didn't wait for her agreement. Without another word he collected his denim jacket from the back of a chair and slammed out.

Claudia stared after him, biting down hard on her lip. With a groan she dropped her forehead against the cushioned back of the couch. He couldn't have made it plainer. Even if he still loved her, and she had seen no sign of it, he had no intention of allowing her a place in his life. As Natalie's mother, she would be tolerated because he had no choice. He would subjugate his emotions to his will. Even if he wanted her, he would never touch her, never go against his own rigid code of ethics. It didn't matter that she was free. That didn't wipe out past sins.

But she had known that, so why did she feel so upset? Surely... surely she wasn't seriously considering fighting for him? It hadn't worked last time—ah, but then he hadn't given her the chance. *Was* she going to fight? Against the ingrained code he had set himself? Is that why she took all his anger and contempt?

It was madness. What would she be fighting for? The answer was simple: the only man she had ever loved, or could ever love. Surely that was worth the gamble? Yet what if he really didn't love her? Somehow in her heart of hearts she just couldn't accept that he didn't, no matter what he said or did. And that was the bare truth of it. No proof, just instinct.

All she had to do was break down the barriers he set up. How was another matter. That could be settled when she had decided whether she was really going to go ahead with it. For at the moment she just didn't know.

With a sigh Claudia shut her eyes on a wave of exhaustion. Her body felt like lead, and her eyes were gritty from lack of sleep. The cushions were warm and inviting. For a moment she fought their pull, for she had things to do, but she was so tired, physically and emotionally. Giving in, she curled up and knew no more.

CHAPTER FIVE

HOURS later Claudia awoke. Her right arm had gone dead, and she felt muzzy and disorientated. Rubbing the offending limb, she winced as the blood rushed painfully back, restoring not only her circulation, but a sense of time and place. She recalled the argument, and Tyler, and instinctively turned her head to see if he had returned.

Not only had he done so, but he was sitting in an armchair, one foot hooked casually over the other knee, watching her. There was a moment, as their eyes met, when time seemed to stand still, and all that had happened earlier hung on the air between them. Then it was as if she could actually see the shutters go down and a deliberate remoteness enter his eyes, making her want to shiver.

She sat up, combing her fingers through her hair. 'What time is it?'

Tyler consulted his watch. 'After one.'

Her head shot up. She'd slept for hours! So long, in fact, that she'd missed visiting Natalie. She could just imagine what her daughter would make of that. Damn it! She needed to make a good impression, not look as if she didn't care. Everything was such a mess!

'You've been to the hospital?' Did she really need to ask? No doubt he thought she was too tired after her assignation to care about her daughter.

'Naturally. Natalie's fine and the doctors are pleased with her. Wendy asked after you,' Tyler informed her casually.

'That was kind of her,' Claudia murmured softly, then dropped her eyes to her hands. 'I don't suppose Natalie even mentioned my name?'

'Not to me, but I overheard her talking to Wendy when I arrived. Apparently Natalie had had the strangest dream. She dreamt she awoke in the night and saw you sitting by her bed.'

Claudia jumped, eyes like huge marbles as she met his gaze. 'But she was asleep!' she protested incredulously.

A strange expression flitted over Tyler's face, in which Claudia recognised anger and confusion. 'So you *were* there. Why the hell didn't you tell me?'

With her secret out, Claudia uttered a brittle laugh. 'You were having too much fun accusing me of sleeping around.'

A muscle jerked in his jaw. 'You have to admit I have every reason to be suspicious,' he argued.

'Oh, please! At least be honest with yourself, Tyler. You don't need a reason. You don't *want* to believe me. I could have a character reference from the Pope, and you'd still accuse me. What are you so afraid of? What possible threat can I be to you?'

'Some women can't help themselves,' he pointed out scornfully.

'And they're more to be pitied than blamed!' Claudia retorted sharply. 'I'm not one of them, Tyler, whatever you think. If you knew anything about my marriage to Gordon you'd know that.'

Tyler straightened in his chair. 'I know you made a commitment to him. Took vows which you broke at the blink of an eye.' His finger stabbed out the point.

Claudia ground her teeth. 'Don't paint Gordon as a white knight. They were the same vows he had already broken so many times that I'd lost count. Whatever he told you, and I can imagine what a tale he spun, Gordon never loved me. He told me that less than a week after we were married. All he wanted was money, but he miscalculated, because it was never mine. When he realised he couldn't get control of it he gave up any pretence of caring.'

Tyler frowned. 'I might be inclined to believe you if you hadn't embarked on a series of affairs of your own.'

'The only "affair" I had was never consummated,' she gritted out as evenly as she could through a mounting anger.

For a moment Tyler looked stunned, then he rallied. 'Oh, come on. Do you seriously expect me to believe that? The newspapers suggested otherwise.'

Claudia stared at him in silence, then jumped to her feet, hands balled into fists in her jeans pockets. She paced unsteadily away, then turned, lips tightly compressed to still their tremble. 'They may have suggested, but there were no affairs, Tyler. Every madcap, dangerous, wild thing they printed I freely admit to doing.' She swallowed hard. 'When you've been told your child is dead, when you believe you've killed her, you have to do something, or go mad. You do anything to forget your overpowering guilt. To be able, for one minute, to forget what you've done. Crazy things, to exhaust you so that you'll sleep for an hour or two.

'But there is no escape, not really, from the knowledge that you should be the one who is

dead, and your child alive! I've bought for-
getfulness. Chased it from country to country,
but always the memory was there, on my
shoulder. There were times I didn't want to
live any more, but even that was denied me.
It was not to be my punishment. That was to
go on living. When you found me I was even
able to forget for weeks at a time. So, you see,
love-affairs were the very last thing I could
have handled, even if I'd wanted them, which
I didn't.'

Her confession tailed off into silence. She
had told him all the agonies that had driven
her these last years. If he didn't believe her
now there was nothing she could say to convince him.

Tyler's eyes never left her face. 'If Gordon
was the liar you say he was why did you believe him?'

Claudia took a painful breath at the memories this brought back. 'Because Natalie was
in the car with me when it crashed,' she revealed in a voice that shook. She saw the
shock wave that went through him as her
words registered. 'He didn't tell you that, did
he? I was leaving him, taking Natalie with me,
but a tyre blew on the motorway...' Even now
the memory brought a cold sweat to her brow.
'When I came to in hospital Gordon was

there. He told me Natalie was dead.' The bitter taste of betrayal made her wince.

'What about the police or the hospital staff? Surely they said something to you?' he probed on, unwilling yet to accept her word.

Claudia closed her eyes, as incredulous now as he at her own gullibility. 'I was in shock, I suppose. If I thought at all I guess I assumed they were all trying to be kind by not mentioning my baby.'

Tyler shook his head in disbelief. 'For God's sake, Claudia. There had to have been a funeral—a death certificate!'

Claudia pressed her hand over her eyes. 'Gordon told me they'd had it while I was in Intensive Care. When I heard that I gave no thought to a certificate. I went crazy. All I wanted to do was die, too. All I could remember was Gordon, with tears in his eyes, telling me my baby was dead.' She looked at him now, eyes awash with tears. 'And it was all lies!'

'My God!' Tyler had gone white. 'Why? Why would he do such a thing?'

'Because he knew I loved her. He knew it would hurt me more than any other thing he could do to take her from me. And he was right. It came close to destroying me utterly. And you don't have to take my word for it.

Ask my family—they'll tell you I'm not lying.'

Tyler pushed himself to his feet, seemed about to say something, then changed his mind. 'Hell!' he swore instead.

'Do you believe me now?'

Tyler stared at a spot on the wall. He spoke almost to himself. 'One night, at dinner, Wendy made a remark about Natalie having been a handful that day. Gordon asked what her favourite toy was, then told Wendy to take it away. Destroy it. That way she'd soon learn to toe the line. He'd been drinking. I thought it was the wine talking. Now I think I understand. He meant it.' Slowly he turned and looked at Claudia. 'Yes, I believe you.'

She swallowed hard on a lump of emotion. 'Thank you.'

Tyler nodded soberly. 'He told me a different story.'

'Gordon wouldn't condemn himself from his own lips. He never expected us to meet again and compare notes,' she said softly. 'You didn't really know your cousin. Not even a quarter as well as Gordon knew you.'

Tyler's face was grim. 'I'm beginning to see that. And the man who brought you home?'

She sighed. 'Was my cousin, Marco. We met quite by accident. I hadn't even known he was in this country. He very kindly offered to drive me home.'

Tyler pulled a disgusted face. 'I see.' One hand rubbed tiredly around his neck. 'You allowed me to believe... what I did.'

Claudia shook her head. 'Not me, Tyler; Gordon. He allowed you to believe I was promiscuous. The same way he allowed me to think that Natalie was dead. Because it was to his advantage. He manipulated everybody. He was very good at it. He needed an ally and you were perfect. He didn't know about us, but he knew of your feelings about erring wives.

'I'm not expecting that to excuse me. I know that, in your eyes, one false step condemns me as if I'd taken hundreds of them. All I'm saying is that I'm not as black as Gordon painted me. The very least you can do is think about it.' Surely he could bend that much?

Blue eyes narrowed on her warily. 'To what end? This changes nothing.'

'I never thought it would. It just seems to me that, for Natalie's sake, we ought to be friends. After all, we'll be seeing a lot of each other from now on,' Claudia ended confidently, reminding Tyler she wasn't leaving.

Tyler laughed, low and self-mocking. 'What a hell of a day!' He glanced her way. 'Whether you and I can ever be friends is debatable, but you're right about Natalie. She needs stability above all things. As we're all she's got, it's up to us to make sure she gets it. We'll give it a try. Just don't expect it to suddenly make Natalie accept you.'

He wasn't telling her anything she didn't know. Natalie felt abandoned by both her parents. She'd been hurt at a very tender age, and she wasn't about to risk being rejected again. It would take time and patience.

But they had made a start today. Tyler hadn't rejected her confession out of hand, as she had fully expected he might. He was, however reluctantly, prepared to meet her halfway, which was all she could hope for when he really didn't trust her, and probably never would. Yet half a loaf, as the old saying went, was better than no bread. It was up to her now to take full advantage of what was on offer, to make her position in Natalie's life unassailable.

To which purpose, a little tardily, she must get her own lawyers to challenge Gordon's will. She wouldn't be denied her legal rights, even if she did eventually temper them to meet Natalie's needs.

First, though, she needed to bathe and change into clean clothes. 'When are you going to the hospital again?'

'I told Wendy about four o'clock. That would give her time to come back here to collect fresh clothes and do whatever it is you women do to titivate yourselves,' Tyler answered after a swift glance at his Rolex. 'Have you had lunch?'

The question reminded her that she hadn't even had breakfast, and her maligned stomach was crying out for food. 'I forgot.'

'You're worse than a baby yourself,' Tyler pronounced, reaching for the telephone.

The snack he ordered was delivered promptly, and Claudia was too ravenous to care that he sat watching her, a mocking curve to his lips, as she tucked in. Replete at last, she sat back with a sigh, licking her fingers.

A burst of male laughter made her heart do a crazy gavotte. She glanced across at Tyler in sheer surprise that he had at last unbent.

'You don't look a day older than Natalie, sitting there. Anyone less elegant and *soignée* I don't think I'm likely to see.'

She laughed back at him, the sudden change lifting her spirits quite dramatically. 'I only feel eight. I've lost years off my life since you told me Natalie was alive. Please don't ever regret it. It was unselfish and generous, and you can never really know what it's meant to me. I have my life back again. For that I'll always be grateful,' she said honestly.

Tyler sobered. 'I don't want your gratitude,' he said stiffly.

That brief moment was gone, but now she had had a glimpse of a softer side which gave her some much needed encouragement. Her smile became wistful. 'I know. But you have it, all the same,' she declared softly, rising gracefully to her feet. 'Be brave. It won't hurt you. It certainly isn't a trap.' She couldn't resist the gibe. How could they ever be friends if he persisted in seeing her as a threat? 'I'm going to bathe and change,' she said, but at the door to the bedroom she paused and looked back at him. Pearly white teeth chewed at her lip. He hadn't asked her why she had been leaving Gordon. Perhaps that had been too much to hope for. At least now, though, he had some inkling what his cousin was like. If it made him think, that was all to the good.

In the meantime she should take things carefully herself, and not get her hopes up. Because reality was that he was right. It really altered nothing where they were concerned. While he held the beliefs he did about cheating wives and mothers, there would always be a wall between them.

With a faint sigh she went to get ready.

Wendy Nicholls greeted them with a smile when they arrived at the hospital later that afternoon. 'I'm afraid Natalie's asleep. She's been dozing on and off all day, but there's nothing to worry about. She'll be much more alert tomorrow. So much so that we'll probably be wishing she'd go to sleep!'

'I'll risk it!' Claudia laughed, looking beyond the young woman to where her daughter lay sleeping peacefully. Warmth flooded her cheeks as she saw the doll she had bought cradled in one slender arm. At least, it appeared, she had done one thing right. That left a mere thousand others that could go disastrously wrong.

'Dr Reardon asked to see you as soon as you arrived, Mr Monroe,' Wendy informed them next. 'I'll gladly wait if Mrs Peterson wants to go with you.'

Claudia felt a chill run up her spine. 'I thought you said Natalie was all right?' she challenged anxiously.

'She is,' Wendy reassured at once. 'I'm sure the doctor only wants to give a progress report. Perhaps even say when he thinks she'll be allowed home.'

Claudia sagged with relief. This was an aspect of motherhood she was going to have to relearn—worrying. Naturally she was willing, but it was rather like being shoved in at the deep end, the circumstances being what they were.

'It's all right, I'll stay with Natalie. You deserve the break, Wendy. Tyler can tell me what the doctor says later.'

Wendy glanced at her watch. 'Well, if you're sure. I do have some shopping to do.'

'Claudia's right,' Tyler put in firmly. 'Off you go now, and don't come back until you're ready.'

The young woman put up no further protest, but gathered together her belongings and departed with a wave. Tyler immediately turned to Claudia, who had crossed to the bed.

'I'll go and see Reardon now. I'll try not to be too long.'

Across the width of the room Claudia fixed him with a steady eye. 'I can manage. Natalie's perfectly safe with me.'

'I wasn't implying otherwise,' he replied irritably. 'I merely thought that if Natalie were to wake up it would be better if I were here too.'

Claudia looked away, grimacing. 'You're right,' she agreed huskily. 'I do seem to upset her, don't I?'

'Are you being wilfully obtuse?' His clipped reply had her head coming up. 'Yes, Natalie's upset, but at least when I'm there I can put the brake on some of the things she says.'

Dumbstruck, Claudia could only manage to utter a faint, 'Oh!'. It was her he sought to protect! The revelation sent her mind spinning dizzily.

Tyler's lips curved mockingly. 'Don't look so surprised. I'm not totally insensitive, you know. If I believe what you said about Gordon then you're even more vulnerable than your daughter.'

His understanding, so totally unexpected, made her defensive. 'I thought you'd be pleased about it. Isn't it what I deserve?' she charged gruffly.

'Perhaps, but I refuse to be used to carry on a dead man's vendetta. To use a child as a pawn is unpardonable. What Natalie needs is permanence. Even a blind man could see you love her.'

His swings kept her continually off balance. 'I don't know what to say.' Surely he couldn't not care and say what he did?

A muscle jerked in his jaw. 'Just don't ever hurt her, Claudia, or you'll be sorry,' he pronounced harshly, then turned abruptly and disappeared down the corridor.

Left alone, Claudia sank on to the nearest chair. He believed her, but she shouldn't read too much into it. He hadn't wanted to trust her, but felt compelled to. Forgiveness was something else. Yet why should she be forgiven for something she hadn't done? She shouldn't, of course, but getting him to believe that might take forever.

What she had now was his friendship, given because she had asked for it, but which now seemed a bitter pill to swallow. It wasn't what she wanted at all. Yet to refuse it was impossible. How would she feel, meeting Tyler often but never having more than his forbearance? Devastated. It was a refinement Gordon would have appreciated. She could only despair.

Claudia rose dejectedly and stepped closer to her sleeping daughter. There was colour in her cheeks now, a healthy colour that boded well. Surely it wouldn't be long before she was allowed home? The probability raised new problems. For home to Tyler and Natalie meant Shropshire. Her concern had been so much for her daughter's health that she hadn't looked beyond the hospital. She looked now, though.

When they went home what happened to her? She didn't even know exactly where his house was, only the county. She would have to find out and start looking for a house somewhere close by. Because one thing was certain: however much Tyler had relented, he wouldn't want her living with him.

She pushed the hurt of that away. She must think positively of what she would have. A home near her daughter where they could begin to rediscover each other. The law, she felt certain, would give over custody to her, but until then they must come to some agreement about visiting. It would be an uphill struggle, but by it she'd prove to Tyler that she could be a responsible parent. Then maybe, just maybe...

Claudia caught herself up in a flight of fancy. Maybe what? He'd forgive her? Love her again? She swallowed hard. They were the sum total of all she wanted. She craved them the way a soul lost in a desert craved water. To give life. Without them she'd be empty, dry. Her passionate nature cried out against the bonds she had to put upon it. Forcing herself to be realistic, she knew at least one of the two was a pipe-dream. The other— well, he might forgive, but never forget.

Yet all of that was the last thing she wanted to think about right now. Most important was finding a way to breach Natalie's under-standable defences. She had no idea of the extent of the damage Gordon's actions had caused, but she was determined to repair it— brick by brick if she had to.

Carefully she bent and brushed her lips over one rosy cheek. She stiffened as Natalie sighed, but didn't wake. Relaxing again, she returned to her chair and made herself com-fortable. There were magazines on a shelf beside her, and she picked one up, beginning to leaf idly through the pages. She wasn't really paying much attention, and so she had gone quite some way past a particular picture when it struck her that there was something familiar about it.

Thumbing back, she smoothed the page and stared at the photograph of a couple sitting side by side on a settee. The sense of familiarity grew, yet she still couldn't place it until she read the caption which named the distinguished white-haired man as the re-nowned pianist Oscar Wheeler, and the extremely chic woman beside him as his wife, Nancy.

Then, of course, she knew. The years had added contentment to the beauty but the face was very much as she had seen it once before in a magazine. This was Nancy, Tyler's mother. Claudia's heart knocked as she swiftly began to read the accompanying article. It was one of a series about women who were wives of famous men, but the fact that struck her the most was that the interview had taken place in London, at the Ritz, where the couple were staying while her husband took part in a series of concerts.

But it didn't say when. Claudia groaned aloud. Sometimes magazines went the rounds for months before being thrown out. Dentists' and doctors' surgeries were notorious for it. She was just about to curse her luck when it belatedly dawned on her to check the front cover. Almost she didn't dare look, yet she forced herself, and what she saw sent her heart thumping. It was the current edition, and that meant that the Wheelers were here, in England, right now.

Claudia found her hands were shaking. For once had the gods decided to come down on her side? It had to be more than coincidence that the woman she most needed to speak to should be here, now. Anxiously she chewed at her lip, frowning. Yes, she wanted to speak to Nancy Wheeler, but would the woman want to speak to her? That possibility hadn't occurred to her before.

Not that she allowed it to depress her for more than a second. She simply wasn't prepared to take no for an answer. There were things about Tyler's past that she had to know, and somehow she *would* know them. First, though, she had to contact the lady, and she couldn't do that while Tyler was present. Which eliminated the hotel, and left only here, at the hospital. It wasn't ideal, but there were pay-phones, for she had seen them.

In an instant she had made up her mind. When Tyler returned she would make some excuse, and slip away to use the telephone.

She was on tenterhooks, waiting for him to come back, but it was almost another half-hour before she heard his footsteps outside the door, and then his tall, athletic figure came in. As usual, her heart lurched at the sight of him, and she couldn't help but remember those passionate minutes in his arms earlier. It brought warm colour to her cheeks, which deepened as he witnessed it with raised brows. There was a light dancing in the back of his eyes that told her he knew exactly what she was thinking.

Yet she refused to look away, lifting her chin instead as he walked towards her. It was only then that she realised she still had the magazine open on her lap, revealing the picture of his mother. She didn't want him to see it, so she closed the page quickly. Too quickly, for the action made him frown.

'You were gone a long time,' she said, vaguely accusing, wanting to divert his attention away from the magazine she now set aside. It worked.

Tyler shrugged, bypassing her to go to the bed and study a now stirring Natalie. 'Dr Reardon had a lot to say.'

'All good, I hope?' she asked, watching Tyler stroke a finger down Natalie's cheek, and experiencing a now familiar twinge of jealousy. Once he had been free with such tender gestures towards her, and she missed them. She wanted his love, the tender moments. Not to have to watch them being reserved for her daughter.

Immediately she hated herself for the unjust emotion. If Tyler loved Natalie she would never deny her daughter the comfort of knowing it. She was just feeling sorry for herself, a state of mind she abhorred.

'Very good,' Tyler finally answered her question. 'All being well, we'll be able to take Natalie home next week.'

Her smile was one of pure joy. 'Oh, Tyler, that's marvellous news,' she cried, jumping up and going to the end of the bed, hands curling around the metal frame. 'I'm so glad.'

'So I see,' he responded, and their eyes met and became locked. A tingling, breathless excitement crackled across the space between them, and it seemed to Claudia that for an aeon she could neither move nor breathe as she was caught in that beam.

What the outcome would have been she would never know, for outside in the corridor someone dropped something heavy and metallic, making them both jump, breaking the spell. In the same instant she saw his unbelievably blue eyes become shuttered once more, closing her out, and her fingers clenched on the cold metal. She knew it was something she'd never get used to.

She cleared her throat. 'I—er—I think I'll go and stretch my legs for a bit.'

His shrug was offhand as he turned his back on her. 'Suit yourself.'

Claudia bit back a scathing retort on his graciousness. She felt buffeted by their see-sawing relationship, never knowing when she would be hitting the highs or sinking to the lows. So she said nothing, but collected her bag and left. Clearly he was regretting having conceded as much as he had. He wouldn't go back on his word, but probably he now thought she had wrought some sort of trick on him! Well, let him think it; she had other fish to fry.

Collecting change for the telephone from one of the gift shops, she made her way to the kiosk that offered the most privacy. Finding the hotel's number was simple enough, but as she waited for her call to be answered her heartbeat increased its pace. By the time the operator was putting her through her nerves were jangling in time with the ring.

'Hello?' A warm feminine voice sing-songed in her ear, and Claudia's mouth went dry.

'Mrs Wheeler?'

'Yes, this is Nancy Wheeler,' the woman concurred, sounding politely curious.

Claudia cleared her throat. 'You don't know me, Mrs Wheeler. My name is Claudia Peterson —— Oh! The pips!' Hastily she broke off and fed more money into the machine. 'Mrs Wheeler?'

'How may I help you, Miss Peterson?' Nancy Wheeler queried cautiously.

'Mrs; it's Mrs Peterson, and ... I'd like to talk to you about your son.'

There was total silence at the other end of the line. When Nancy Wheeler spoke again the friendliness had turned to wariness. 'My ... son?'

'Yes, Tyler. Tyler Monroe,' Claudia enlarged, feeling her own tension mount with that of the woman at the other end.

'How did you know he was my son?' The voice cracked a little.

Claudia closed her eyes. 'He told me. There was a photo of you and your husband once, in a magazine. You'd just been married. Oh!' The pips went again and she fed the hungry beast impatiently. 'This is vitally important to me, Mrs Wheeler. I need your help.'

The voice at the other end strove for calmness. 'If you know who I am then you also know I haven't seen my son for over twenty years. I'm not the one who can help you.'

There was a finality there that warned Claudia the other woman was about to ring off, and she hurried into speech. 'Oh, you're wrong! You're the *only* one who can. You see, I love him, Mrs Wheeler. But ——'

'My dear, I have no influence over my son. If he doesn't love you ——'

'But he does!' Claudia interrupted quickly. 'That is, he did, and perhaps he would again if he allowed himself. You see, I was leaving my husband when I met Tyler. When he found out he wouldn't listen to my reasons. He despises me for breaking my vows.'

A soft, almost pained sigh echoed down the line. 'I think I begin to see.'

'I won't give up without a fight, but I can't fight what I don't know.' Suddenly the decision she had hesitated over had been made.

Nancy Wheeler drew an audible breath. 'It was such a long time ago.'

'Not for Tyler,' Claudia added softly.

There was silence for a moment or two. 'Very well. I have a busy schedule, but I'm free for lunch tomorrow. Can you join me here at one o'clock?'

Claudia was swept by a wave of relief. 'I'll be there, and thank you for agreeing to see me, Mrs Wheeler.' She replaced the receiver slowly. Well, she had negotiated the first hurdle, but not without some difficulty. Her call must have opened up some very deep wounds, yet she knew of no other way. To win she had to use all her ingenuity. She prayed in the end it would be worth it.

Natalie was awake and sitting up eating her tea when Claudia returned. The sound of her daughter's cheerful laugh brought a smile to her lips as she entered the room.

'Well, you sound much better,' she declared brightly, drawing up another chair beside the bed. 'How do you feel?'

Natalie's laughter died away as she regarded her mother with a curious look in her eye. 'Sore,' she answered quietly.

Claudia half reached out her hand, then drew it back again, fearing rejection. Natalie seemed to freeze and Claudia's smile faltered a little as she wished she hadn't stopped, but it was too late now. 'I bet you are, but it will soon go away. Then you'll be going home. I expect you're looking forward to that, aren't you?' she rallied.

The young girl fiddled with her spoon. 'I guess so,' she agreed with a shrug.

Claudia darted a questioning glance at Tyler, then looked back at Natalie. 'You don't sound too sure. I thought you'd be delighted to go home with Tyler.'

Natalie glared. 'Of course I am. I love Tyler, and he loves me!' she insisted forcefully.

Claudia dropped her lashes, speared by a shaft of pure jealousy. She mastered it with an effort, but her smile was tight. 'Then that makes you a very lucky girl.' I wish I could say the same for myself, she added silently.

Her daughter's face took on a pugnacious look as she added, 'I know. I don't need a mummy or daddy, 'cos I've got Tyler.'

Tyler's voice drowned out Claudia's pained gasp. 'Nevertheless, you do have a mother, and that makes you twice as lucky. Mothers are special people.'

He had caught the girl's attention. 'Why?'

Claudia gazed at him in stupefaction. Considering his views on mothers in general, and his own in particular, this was quite an about-face.

'Because they love you and forgive you, no matter what you do or say.'

The statement brought a lump to her throat. He was putting himself fully behind her, just as he had said he would. Her ally in this, if in no other thing. The sadness came from knowing he didn't really believe it. They were just words. He was relying on her not to let him down even as he expected she would. For mothers were not to be trusted. He had no faith, and trust died without it. Somehow she had to find a way to change that.

The effect of his words on Natalie was re-strained: doubt warred on her young face, yet she didn't immediately disregard them. Instead she fell silent, thinking. Claudia hoped it was a good omen.

They stayed for another hour, only leaving when Wendy returned. Claudia hugged to herself the knowledge that, while not being overly enthusiastic, Natalie's farewell had been unprompted. That had to be because of Tyler's intervention. The truth was that he could have swayed Natalie either way, such was his standing in her daughter's eyes. That he had chosen to back her was a shift in mood that had her turning to him as they drove back to the hotel.

'Thank you for saying what you did back there.'

Tyler didn't take his eyes off the road ahead. 'Don't read more into it than was intended,' he warned calmly.

Claudia sat back in her seat, the night seeming to darken around her. 'Why is it so hard to accept anything from me? Even gratitude?' she queried irritably.

'Because it makes me wonder what you expect to get in return.'

Fighting his constant suspicion was like hitting her head against a brick wall! 'I already have it,' she snapped.

He laughed. 'You're very touchy.'

Her breath drew in sharply. 'Don't play games, Tyler! This means too much to me to be funny! Perhaps it amuses you to have me rushing around like a chicken with its head cut off, but I only have this one chance with Natalie and I can't afford to waste it. You know damn well I need all the help you can give me. So if you've decided not to believe me, despite everything I've told you, then tell me. Or do you simply enjoy watching me squirm?' Claudia shot back angrily, tired of this continuous fencing.

Tyler released a deep breath. 'You can relax, Claudia. I believe Gordon lied. It sticks in my craw that he used me, and like a fool I let him.'

Claudia shivered, despite the balmy night. 'He used everyone. I knew it, but I stayed with him. That was my weakness. I was too proud to admit I'd made a mistake, and he knew it.'

'Yet by your own admission you *did* leave,' he countered.

'Even now, knowing what he was like, would you still have had me stay?' she asked incredulously.

'The marriage service says for better or worse. You can't opt out when the going gets tough,' Tyler pointed out.

'That's positively medieval!' Claudia exclaimed. 'Must we be condemned for life for one mistake? You don't know what it was like being married to Gordon!'

'And I don't want to know,' he retorted levelly, keeping his attention fixed firmly on the road. 'You know my feelings. They haven't changed.'

Bitter tears burned the backs of her eyes. 'Then you're a fool, Tyler,' she declared thickly. 'There's little enough happiness in this world. We have to grasp it when we can. We aren't often given a second chance.'

'You can be damn sure my father wasn't!' he agreed with a savage laugh.

There was no way she could bite back her angry reply. 'But he could have had. He had you, Tyler! There was a life before him, but instead he drank himself to death. I don't suppose you ever asked yourself why, either! You say it was because he longed for your mother to come back, but I'm wondering if it wasn't more likely to have been out of guilt.'

Tyler braked the car so sharply that Claudia had to fling out a hand against the dashboard to save herself. There was murder in his eyes when he looked at her.

'My God, you little bitch, I could kill you for that! My father lived for that woman. He worshipped the ground she walked on. He gave her everything she could ever want!' Gripped about the steering-wheel, his hands were white-knuckled.

His anger bombarded her, but, though it dried her mouth, Claudia refused to be quelled. 'If that was so,' she challenged huskily, 'why did she leave? There had to be a reason.'

His lip curled, making his face ugly in its derision. 'Sure there was—pure greed. Once she'd sucked him dry she went off in search of greener pastures.'

'And left you,' she ended softly, not meaning him to hear, but he did, and the temperature dropped dramatically.

'What the hell does that mean?'

She had to go on, for she had said too much. She licked her lips nervously, following an instinctive reasoning she hadn't fully investigated herself. 'Are you sure all this anger is for your father? Isn't it really for you? Because she left you behind?'

'Are you accusing me of being some kind of mummy's boy?' he demanded with awesome quiet.

Claudia shook her head impatiently. 'No, of course not. But you were young, and you were hurt——' His fist crashed down on the console, cutting her off abruptly.

'Enough! I don't need your mawkish amateur psychology. I was never hurt, because she could never hurt me. All she did was help me to grow up fast. For which I suppose I should be thanking her.'

Claudia felt a desperate need to cry. For the boy that he had been. Who had suffered hurt he denied, and was still hurting—even if he didn't know it. More than ever she knew her meeting with his mother was vital. Nancy Wheeler held the key to so many doors. Doors that needed to be opened so that the truth could come out. So that the past could finally be laid to rest and they could all look forward to the future. She refused to believe it was too late.

A seething silence accompanied the rest of the journey back to the hotel. But, instead of parking the car, Tyler dropped her off at the door with a muttered remark that he had someone to see, and drove off, leaving her abandoned on the pavement, staring after the departing tail-lights helplessly.

She ordered dinner in their suite, but barely did justice to the excellently prepared meal. Nor could she concentrate on the film she discovered as she flicked through the television channels. Her mind constantly veered back to Tyler. What was he doing? Where was he? Especially as the hours ticked by and he still hadn't returned. He had been angry enough to get drunk, but she doubted, given his background, that that was one of his vices. So where was he? Who was this person he had had to see? Could it be a woman?

Her heart sank. Why not? She doubted if he had spent the last six years in abstinence. He had always been a physical man. A sensual man. Women would be an essential part of his life.

The idea of him being with a lover now brought a wave of jealousy ripping through her, making her gasp. It didn't matter that he was free to do as he pleased; the mere thought that he could be making love to her as he had to herself that morning made Claudia feel sick.

She tried to banish the visions her mind conjured up by taking a shower, but they remained to torture her long after she had climbed into bed. As she lay sleepless in the darkness she knew she had no right to be jealous. She had lost Tyler a long time ago. But her heart refused to listen. She knew it always would, because in her heart she had always been faithful to him. To have had an affair would have been inconceivable.

They belonged together—were made for each other. That was why she was going to see his mother. She was fighting for her future, and the implications of failure were too bitter to contemplate.

CHAPTER SIX

CLAUDIA stepped into the opulent sur-
roundings of the Ritz at precisely five minutes
to one the following afternoon, and approached the desk with a sense of having
burnt her boats. She had dressed carefully in
a favourite Lagerfeld creation, the dusky pink
silk of the dress and matching bolero jacket
flattering her colouring. It added colour, too,
to a face that was pale from lack of sleep. She
had tossed and turned for hours before Tyler
had finally returned, and what sleep she had
had then had been disturbed.

Careful make-up had been a necessity. At
least it gave her the outward semblance of
calm, and had served to hide from him the
tell-tale signs of her restlessness. Tyler hadn't
explained his prolonged absence, and she had
bitten back her own demands to know where
he had been. It had tried her patience sorely
when he had observed her with barely con-
cealed mockery. Clearly he hadn't forgiven
her for her comments yesterday, and had been
waiting for an opportunity to say something
crushing.

She hadn't given him the chance, opting for a studied indifference, informing him instead that she had arranged to meet her cousin Marco for lunch. It had been an inspired idea, and one he hadn't queried. Thus she had been able to walk into the hotel confident that he hadn't the slightest inkling who she was really visiting.

She waited patiently until a clerk was free, then gave her name. 'Mrs Wheeler is expecting me.'

The young man consulted a list. 'Ah, yes, Mrs Peterson. You're to go straight up.'

No more than a couple of minutes later Claudia was raising a hand to knock on the door. The woman who opened it was something of a surprise. That this was Tyler's mother Claudia had no doubt, yet she was shorter and plumper than she had imagined. Somehow her voice had given the impression of a tall, *soignée* woman, whereas in reality she was the opposite.

'Mrs Peterson?' Nancy Wheeler smiled, but Claudia could see the paleness of tension in her cheeks. There were shadows in her remarkable blue eyes and a tightness to her lips that talked of a rigid control. 'Do come in.' She led the way inside the elegantly furnished room. 'Sit down, won't you? I've ordered lunch to be served up here later, for it would be more private.' She sat down, smoothing the material of her dress over her knees in a betrayingly nervous gesture, and indicated that Claudia should take the couch opposite.

'I half expected you to have changed your mind,' Claudia said as she made herself comfortable. She had to know what type of woman she faced.

Nancy Wheeler gave her a level look that reminded Claudia uncannily of her son. 'To be perfectly frank, I almost did. But I had a long talk with my husband, Oscar, and he convinced me that this was the right thing to do.'

Claudia shifted uneasily in her seat. 'I appreciate that this may be upsetting for you. Please believe me, I wouldn't be asking if I didn't think it was important. Not just to me, but to Tyler, too,' Did she care?

Nancy Wheeler glanced down to where her fingers toyed with the rings on her left hand. 'How is he?'

There was a wealth of agony hidden behind those three simple words, and Claudia felt it, because it mirrored her own anguish at the loss of her child. That didn't speak of a woman who had callously abandoned her family. This wasn't the woman Tyler described at all.

'He's well. He's a son you can be proud of,' she declared gently.

The older woman looked up, her smile wry. 'I am proud. My son's career is one that I follow religiously. I've always admired his instinct for success.'

'So... you didn't turn away from him?' The question had to be asked.

Again that level look came her way. 'I love my son, Mrs Peterson. If I didn't we wouldn't be having this conversation.'

'I'm sorry, but I had to know,' she apologised ruefully. 'I love him too.'

'So you told me. And you need my help.'

Claudia leaned forward, hands pressed together as she marshalled her thoughts. 'I don't even know if it will do any good. I only know I have to try. You see, I met Tyler eight years ago, and we fell in love. I've loved him ever since.' She sighed heavily. 'He loved me too. I truly believe that he did, but he left me. One day he showed me a picture of you and your husband and said something that... It's a very complicated story, but I'd better start right at the beginning. The day I met Gordon Peterson, my husband.'

It wasn't easy to relate all that had happened. The narrative brought back painful memories, but Claudia withheld nothing. There was a kind of catharsis in the telling that finally eased the many heartaches, and left her exhausted but at peace with herself. Through it all Nancy Wheeler listened in an ever-deepening silence, horrified and disgusted by turns at the revelations, her eyes, deeply compassionate, never leaving that downbent head.

When it was over neither moved for a while, then Nancy rose and went to pour two measures of brandy. She handed one to Claudia, who accepted it gratefully, then resumed her seat, waiting patiently until the younger woman sighed and rested back against the cushions.

'I'm sorry, my dear, that you had to go through all that. I had no idea of exactly how Tyler reacted to my leaving. Oh, I expected him to be hurt, but not to that extent. The separation was never intended to be permanent. Events went beyond my control. I wrote and explained. I wrote him many letters those first few years, but I never received any replies.'

Claudia frowned. 'But he never received any letters.'

For a moment his mother looked surprised and then she said in an odd voice, 'Did he write to me?'

'He told me he did,' Claudia confirmed, and watched a shaft of pain cross the other woman's face.

'I see. Funny, but I never considered... I thought perhaps it was his father's influence.'

Claudia was lost. 'What happened?'

There was a bitter edge to Nancy Wheeler's smile. 'I sent my letters to Tyler's grandparents' home. He was living with them. They never did like me. Now I see they must have destroyed my letters and Tyler's. My God, how could they? To think of him now, so warped and bitter. Denying himself love, and all because... What a terrible, terrible waste of a life!'

There were tears in the other woman's eyes that she dabbed at inadequately with her fingers. Claudia's heart went out to her, and in an instant she was on the other couch, taking one trembling hand in hers.

'Please, won't you tell me what happened?' she urged.

Nancy Wheeler patted Claudia's hand and smiled moistly. 'Perhaps if I do the past will finally lie down and rest. I met Tyler's father in Africa. He owned a farm there, from where he ran a modest safari outfit. He was handsome and dashing and I think I fell in love with the whole adventure of the thing as much as I did with Kit. I went to Africa on safari, and I stayed on as a wife.

'At first everything was perfect. I didn't mind the isolation, for I had Kit, and then Tyler came along. We were ecstatically happy—or so I thought. There were always people coming and going. While Kit ran the animal side of things, I took on the catering and running of the lodge. We were very successful, but I think that's what started to destroy our marriage. You see, I had always known that Kit was a jealous man, a possessive man. Almost from the first he resented his son because he took up so much of my time. Yet I think we would have survived that if only the hunting lodge hadn't been there.

'I had to mix with the guests, for that was part of my job, and the proportion of men to women was generally about three to one. At first I laughed off Kit's suspicions, but it got so that I couldn't even talk to a man about breakfast without him accusing me of having an affair. It soon grew impossible. He'd make excuses to come back to the homestead to check up on me. He'd radio in whenever he could, and if I should be breathless because I'd run to answer it you can guess what he thought was going on.

'It was awful. He started calling me vile names, and his accusations grew wilder. He became something of a laughing-stock, and the business began to suffer. There were fights with guests—all manner of things. I didn't know what to do, where to turn. My only family were in England. I had no money of my own. Kit had alienated me from any friends I had tried to make. His jealousy was slowly but surely driving me out of my mind. Fortunately Tyler was at boarding-school during the worst of it. I didn't want him to know what was going on. I had no fears that Kit would harm him in any way, but I did worry that his wild accusations would turn my son against me. Kit would have liked that, to know I had nobody but him.

'Anyway, it got so bad that I knew the only way to save my sanity was to leave. I had truly loved Kit, and I believe he had loved me, but his jealousy had destroyed it. There was no question of divorce. He would never have let me go. One day, when Kit was away, I packed a case, took the car, and left. I planned to collect Tyler and take him home to my family. I'd get the money somehow.

'Only it never happened. I reached a friend's house, one of the few I still had, and collapsed. I spent the next months in a sanatorium. When I left the hospital I discovered that Tyler had left school and was living with his father. It was more than I dared do to go back there. I found work and a place to live.

'Kit took to drink, and I suppose poor Tyler listened to all his ramblings about my ingratitude. How I'd taken everything and left, abandoning them both. What else would a ten-year-old believe when he doesn't hear from his mother for six months?' There was no bitterness in Nancy Wheeler's voice, only a deep sadness.

'What did you do?' Claudia prompted.

The older woman sighed. 'All that I could do. I arranged to write to Tyler via my in-laws, then I started to rebuild my life as best I could. Of course, it hurt when I didn't hear from my son, but I just kept on writing. When I heard Kit had died and that Tyler was with Kit's parents I did try to see him, but they told me Tyler didn't want to see me, that he wanted to have nothing to do with me, and that if I was wise I'd leave him alone and allow him to mourn his father. What else could I do? I believed he was happy there. He didn't want me. I believed there would come a time for explanations. So I did as they asked, trusting that one day my son would seek me out. I always made sure my in-laws knew where I could be contacted. But he never did. I spent a lot of years living in hope, until good friends convinced me that I must start to live for myself. They were right, of course. In the end I left Africa—the rest, as they say, is history.'

The two women stared at each other, appalled and saddened by a tragedy that need never have happened, but which, like a recurring nightmare, seemed about to happen again.

'He has to be told the truth,' Claudia declared determinedly.

'Oh, I agree wholeheartedly,' Nancy Wheeler responded immediately. 'I always wanted to see him, but as the years went by somehow it became more and more impossible. If only I'd had the courage I could have spared him all this terrible anger. I thought what I was doing was for the best. His grandparents loved him, he was happy, whereas there were times when I barely had enough to eat or keep a roof over my head. I couldn't have cared for him the way they did, not in the beginning.' She sighed heavily. 'My poor, poor Tyler.'

She sank back against the cushions, her thoughts many years away.

A polite knock at the door failed to breach the older woman's thoughts, and so it was Claudia who answered it and allowed the waiter in with their lunch. Only when he'd left, after efficiently laying the table, did she stir. There was a glint of determination in her eye as she looked at Claudia.

'My son has hated me for over twenty years, and it's gone on long enough. I intend to tell him the truth and make an end of it.'

'But how? Where? Tyler's proud and stubborn. He isn't prepared to listen,' Claudia argued, knowing only too well the enormity of the task.

Nancy Wheeler rose to her feet. 'It's up to me to make him listen. What I can't force him to do is believe me. That won't help your cause, will it? You have a great deal to tell him yourself.'

'I have my pride, too. He's got to ask me. I have to know that he wants to know. We both know he'll never do that unless he hears from you.'

'And perhaps not even then.' Nancy Wheeler took Claudia's arm. 'You'll have to brace yourself for the possibility.'

Claudia smiled wanly. 'At the moment Tyler despises me. I don't know if he does or could feel anything else, so I've nothing to lose.'

'Neither have I.' Nancy Wheeler returned the smile generously. 'Mrs Peterson, we seem to be two women with a mission—to redeem my son. When we succeed, and if things turn out the way we both want them to, I'll have great joy in welcoming you into my family. Therefore I intend to call you Claudia, if I may. I hope you have no objections to calling me Nancy?'

'None at all.'

'Good,' Nancy declared briskly. 'Let's eat. I didn't think I'd be able to, but now I feel famished. We have plans to make.'

Seated at the table in the window, they helped themselves from an array of salad dishes. Claudia was amazed to find she had quite an appetite too. It was some little time before either spoke again. Then it was Nancy who said thoughtfully, 'The only real difficulty is when to see Tyler. I wouldn't dream of it while your daughter is still in hospital. Oscar's London concerts finish in two days anyway. We have to go on to Glasgow, Edinburgh and then Manchester. We won't be back here for some time.' Her fingers tapped out a tattoo on the table-top.

'Manchester?' Claudia said quickly, 'Tyler lives somewhere in Shropshire. That's not far away. He'll be taking Natalie there as soon as she's well enough.'

'My dear, that would be perfect. If I can catch him when you and Natalie are there he can hardly cause a scene, can he?' Nancy pulled a wry face.

Claudia jabbed her fork into a juicy prawn. 'Actually, I don't know where I'll be. That is, I'll have to find somewhere to live close by. But I promise I'll help in any way I can. If you give me the number where you'll be staying, and when, I'll ring you as soon as the time is right.'

Nancy frowned. 'But surely you'll be living with your daughter?'

'That would be difficult. All Gordon's actions are questionable. I rang my lawyer this morning and he's going to contest the will. I could probably get temporary custody of Natalie until the court rules, but I wouldn't dream of that right now, when she's been in hospital. She'll convalesce better in a place she knows, and that's Tyler's home. I hardly think he will want me in his house.'

Nancy shook her head in irritation. 'I never met your husband, or any of the Petersons. They could only be distant relatives of Kit's. I'm glad I never did, and you can't know how sorry I am that Tyler met him. The vindictiveness leaves me speechless. It's inconceivable that Tyler could have been so taken in, despite everything.'

Claudia winced. 'Gordon was a charmer, so clever at manipulating people. They met at university, and I suppose Gordon said all the right things and Tyler unburdened himself. On any other subject Tyler wouldn't have been so susceptible. We're his blind spot, I'm afraid.'

'Perhaps there's some sort of divine plan behind all the suffering we've gone through. Heaven knows, if I had stayed in Africa I wouldn't have met my second husband, the actor Donald Miles. We had seven years together. Bitter-sweet years, because he was already suffering from cancer when I married him. When I lost him I never expected to meet anyone else, but then Oscar came along and transformed my life. I don't believe I've ever been so happy and contented. None of this would have happened if Kit hadn't been such a jealous man. Not that I wouldn't have sacrificed everything to keep my son, only that was not to be. Yet, when I'd given up all hope of seeing him again, you come into my life and give me the chance of reaching him. There has to be a power behind it. Something we can't see but can only follow, with faith.'

Claudia smiled. 'It's a comforting thought, but I'd be happier if Tyler felt it too.'

'Perhaps he does. Who knows? You said he was stubborn, and I take your word for it. I know very little about my son, but that is something, God willing, that's about to change.' Nancy sipped from a glass of white wine. 'Tell me about him, Claudia; everything you know, however small.'

They spent the next hour talking about their children and making tentative plans. It wasn't just their similar plight that brought them together; there was an empathy too. Claudia liked Nancy Wheeler very much. There was a great deal of her son in her. Yet that had no bearing on the friendship she felt. The age difference meant nothing. They would always have been friends when they met.

Claudia left the hotel feeling much lighter of heart at having shared her burden. What Nancy had told her made her understand Tyler so much better, but there still seemed no easy solution to the problem. Yet even that couldn't take the spring out of her step.

Somehow she would use what she knew to her advantage.

It was a lovely afternoon, and she decided to walk back, doing a little shopping on the way, entering one of the large department stores to pick out a few books she hoped Natalie might enjoy. They had been favourites of her own, and their appeal was universal.

She was pleasantly tired when she finally took the lift up to their suite. There would be time for a relaxing bath and a cup of tea before going to the hospital again. Tyler hadn't said he was going out, but somehow Claudia wasn't expecting him to be in when she let herself into the room. He was there, though, slouched comfortably in an armchair, talking to someone else, who brought her up short. Smiling at her from another chair was her cousin Marco.

Her smile faltered, eyes shooting to Tyler, whose lips curved in a greeting that singularly failed to reach his own eyes.

'Look who came to visit,' he said smoothly.

Caught out in a blatant lie, Claudia licked her lips. 'Hello, Marco, have you been here long?' Brain working fast, she walked further into the room and accepted the affectionate kiss of greeting he rose to plant on her cheek.

'About half an hour,' Tyler answered for him. 'I insisted he waited. I knew you'd be pleased to see him.'

The underlying threat made her heart leap. Sitting down and laying her packages aside, Claudia took time to regain her poise. 'It's a lovely surprise. What brings you here, Marco?'

His white smile flashed out. 'You, as always, *cara*. But seriously, I had a telephone call from Aunt Lucia. She asked me to find out how you were, and to find a gift for Natalie.' He brought a small packet from his pocket and passed it to her. 'It's nothing much, just something to wish her well.'

'Thank you, Marco,' Claudia said warmly, 'I'm sure she'll love it. But you shouldn't have gone to such trouble.'

He waved a hand. 'For you and your family, Claudia, nothing is too much. Also I came to pass on a reminder to get in touch with our aunt. She said she hasn't heard from you.'

'I know; I should have telephoned, but things have been rather hectic. I promise I'll write as soon as I can.'

Her cousin nodded. *'Bene.'*

Tyler broke his watchful silence as the cousins smiled at each other. 'Marco and I have been trying to work out who you were having lunch with. A relative, you told me, but I forget the name. Who was it now?' His tone was a masterful blend of self-irritation and mild interest, which successfully hid from all but Claudia that he was blazingly angry.

Marco unwittingly added fuel to the fire. 'Yes, *cara*, who is it? Giancarlo and Anna aren't due until next month. Is it Raf?' He mentioned the names of his brothers and sister-in-law.

Claudia could have groaned aloud. If only Marco hadn't chosen to call today! Still, there was no point in involving him further. Tyler hadn't seen fit to tell him of her lie, for which she supposed she should be grateful. Except she knew his reasoning was in no way altruistic. He wanted to challenge her on her own. An interview she'd give her eye-teeth to delay if she could. Meanwhile...

'I do have other relatives,' she said pointedly. 'My Uncle George was over from America. He needed my signature on a document. He was as prosey as ever, and afterwards I cheered myself up with some shopping. Fancy you forgetting George's name, Tyler.' She couldn't resist the taunt.

His eyes flashed. 'Hmm, yes, fancy.'

Soft colour washed into her cheeks, making her grateful for Marco's interruption.

'He's the stuffy one who looks after your investments. I met him once, didn't I?'

'That's right. Whatever his faults, he certainly knows how to look after my holdings.'

Tyler broke in with a laugh. 'Investments? Holdings? With your lifestyle I shouldn't imagine there's very much of your divorce settlement left!'

'Settlement —— ' Marco began, but Claudia held up a hand to cut him off.

She regarded Tyler coldly. 'So Gordon told you about that, did he? What he didn't tell you was that I can handle money with the best of them.' She had discovered another lie and wanted to know just how far it went.

'Doing what you like with pin money hardly makes you a financial wizard,' Tyler drawled mockingly.

'An attitude once shared by my great-uncles. Perhaps you know nothing about them. I thought they were common knowledge, but I suppose Gordon thought it best not to mention them. He wanted your sympathy, not your condemnation, and, with your financial background, you might just have linked them to the Webster heiresses.'

Tyler sat up straighter, eyes narrowing. 'Webster heiresses? Are we talking about the Wall Street Websters?'

Claudia smiled grimly. Gordon had been right to be cautious, for Tyler had heard of them. 'We are. How much do you know about them?'

He was clearly trying to make the connection. 'Not much. There were two girls, orphaned in the same accident. There was a great splash about it when one of them died a few years ago. What were their names, now? Old-fashioned ones, as I recall. Amelia! That was the one who died, and the other was...' He tailed off, eyes locking with hers in disbelief.

'Claudia,' she supplied. 'It's actually quite funny when you think about it. You both didn't want to remember that name. You because... well, *because*, and Gordon because, having married the wrong cousin for her money, he discovered that his ex-wife, from whom he had received a substantial divorce settlement, had become the heiress after all. That really must have stung!'

Tyler shot to his feet and took a turn about the room before returning to stand before her. '*You* are Claudia Webster? No wonder you can afford to flit around the world doing much as you please.'

What else had she expected? There was no railing at Gordon's lack of honesty, only a disparagement of her own behaviour. 'I could, but I don't any more. Yes, I go around the world, but with a purpose. I run several charitable foundations for underprivileged children. We send missions to the Third World countries to offer aid. It takes up a great deal of time. Perhaps you've heard of us, the Webster Foundation?'

He swore. 'Who hasn't?' he exclaimed, but there was a new respect in his eyes. 'That's your baby?'

'Mm-hmm. As I said, it's an exacting business. So when I can I do let my hair down.'

'And get into the papers,' Tyler finished, without a trace of mockery.

'The paparazzi! What do they know or care?' Marco exploded in her defence. 'Scandal is all they're interested in. But we know better, eh, *cara*?' He held out his hand to her, which she took gratefully, but his eyes were on Tyler, daring him to comment otherwise.

Tyler's expression at this championing was mildly humorous. 'I'm not arguing. It just that what Claudia has told me takes some getting used to. My cousin led me to believe that Claudia was penniless.'

Marco said something obscene in Italian. 'That one was so crooked that he could hide behind a corkscrew!'

Eyes dancing, Claudia looked at Tyler to see how he would take this defamation of his spotless cousin. Tyler didn't laugh, but neither did he rush to defend, and that was something in itself. He looked thoughtful, and Claudia mentally crossed her fingers. Changing tack, she looked at her cousin.

'I have a wonderful idea. Why don't you come to the hospital with us and give Natalie her present yourself? I'm sure she'd enjoy that, and you know how wonderful you are with children. Do say you'll come, Marco,' she urged.

As she had known, he didn't hesitate. 'If I won't be in the way.'

Claudia glanced over at Tyler, whose eyes had narrowed once more in suspicion. 'It's all right, isn't it?'

He seemed about to argue, and she realised he thought she was trying a delaying tactic. It wasn't deliberate, even if it was fortuitous, but she couldn't stop him thinking what he liked.

'Perfectly all right. Do you want to change? If not, we may as well go,' was all he finally said, the implication being that the sooner the visit was over, the sooner they could have their talk.

'I'll go as I am,' she smiled blithely, although her heart quaked. From the look on his face he knew exactly how she was feeling, and enjoyed having her on the defensive once more.

After an initial bout of shyness Natalie was delighted with her new cousin. He was at ease with her, teasing her outrageously, as he did his own nephews and nieces. He flirted with Wendy and the other nurses, and was such a hit that Natalie even lost her reserve with her mother, thanking her genuinely for the books, which Cousin Marco had to read from, naturally.

They had to leave eventually, dropping her cousin off at his club before heading back to the hotel.

'I'm surprised your cousin doesn't have children of his own,' Tyler remarked as they waited at some traffic lights.

'He would have done, I expect, but his fiancée was killed in a riding accident eighteen months ago,' Claudia explained with a heavy sigh. 'I guess you could say he's still running from his own ghosts. A light went out for him that day; it's going to take an exceptional woman to turn it back on.'

Tyler put the car in gear as the lights changed. 'What does he do?'

'Believe it or not, he's a lecturer in pre-Columbian art. At the moment he's on holiday.'

'Is anybody in your family what they seem to be?' Tyler growled ruefully.

Claudia gave a half-smile. 'Did you take him for a dilettante? You're a great one for jumping to conclusions.'

'And you ——' Tyler began, only to bite back the words. 'You,' he went on more softly, 'are a liar, my dear Claudia.'

Which statement had her biting her lip and turning away in silence. A silence that lasted until they were once more in their suite, the door shut and guarded as Tyler leant back against it. The moment Claudia had dreaded was to be put off no longer.

'So, who did you have lunch with, Claudia?' Tyler asked in a voice as smooth and velvety as chocolate.

Keeping a careful distance between them, she swung to face him. 'I don't have to account for my movements to you, Tyler,' she pointed out defensively.

'Then why bother to lie?' he challenged back, pushing away from the door and advancing on her. 'You may as well tell me, for I mean to know. You won't be leaving here until I do.'

He meant it. There was determination in every tense line of his body. Claudia debated with herself over the best course of action. She could lie, but she had the uncanny feeling he'd know it. Which left her with the truth. There really didn't seem much point in concealing it now, so she squared her shoulders.

'If you must know, I had lunch with your mother,' she told him baldly.

Tyler went absolutely rigid. 'You *what*?' The question would have been a yell if it hadn't almost been whispered.

A little unnerved, but still defiant, Claudia tried to be blasé. 'I had lunch with your mother,' she repeated with a shrug, which tailed off abruptly as he caught her by the shoulders.

'You interfering little ——' Tyler bit the words back with a growl of disgust. 'Who the hell gave you the right to pry into my private affairs? Sneaking around behind my back!'

Claudia brought her hands up, pushing uselessly against his chest. 'How am I to know anything if you won't tell me?' she argued, wincing as his fingers cut in tighter.

'You know all you need to know. Stay out of my past. Do you hear me, Claudia? Keep your nose out of things that don't concern you. Things you don't understand!' he warned chillingly.

'But I *do* understand. It's you who doesn't,' she insisted. 'She wants to see you. To explain.'

Tyler laughed. 'Explain? Once I was foolish enough to believe her lies. That won't happen again. I learn by my mistakes.'

'You're making one now.'

'Not in my book. My mother chose her path and I chose mine. They don't meet and never will.'

Her eyes pleaded with him. 'They could if you'd just bend a little.'

With a faint sigh Tyler released her. 'Listen, Claudia. I know that finding Natalie means a lot to you, and consequently you want everyone to be just as happy, but life isn't like that. You mean well, I suppose, but it's too late. We have nothing to say to each other. So no more. Let it go.' He shot back his cuff to consult his watch. 'Now I must dash; I have a date for dinner.'

After the disappointment of that exchange, to be abandoned for a second night had her eyes lurching to his, and she was unable to bite back the rash words that sprang to her lips. 'Who with? A woman?' She could have died at the bitter way they emerged, for Tyler picked up on it at once.

'What if it is? Jealous, Claudia?' His eyes glittered mockingly. 'I've just got through telling you my life is my own. Who I choose to dine with is my affair.' Crossing to the bedroom door, he glanced back. 'I use the term advisedly.' He added the rider before disappearing.

Dispirited, Claudia sank on to the nearest chair. Her confession had achieved absolutely nothing—except alienating him even further. He was unreasonable and obstinate—and she just didn't know what to do next. She had been a fool to let him see that she cared what he did, or with whom, for he would use it to ward her off if she ever tried to probe again. It was all just one unholy mess!

An hour later Tyler left without a word, save to advise her not to wait up. She gave him a glower which bounced off his back like indiarubber. As the door closed she decided that she wouldn't sit in their room wondering and worrying. She had too much pride. Instead she washed and changed into a violet silk cocktail dress and went down to dinner in the restaurant.

More than one male head turned at her appearance, which boosted her flagging morale, but there was really no fun in dining in lonely splendour. So she didn't linger after all, but returned to the suite. A documentary on one of the Egyptian tombs held her interest for a while, but the film she had seen already. She watched it with only half her attention, growing restless and edgy as the hours ticked by.

Her thoughts drifted to Tyler. Whoever he was dining with, it surely didn't take this long. No, he was making a point. Using a sledgehammer to prove to her that she had no place in his life. In fact, all she really had was Natalie, and she wasn't even sure of her! A heaviness settled about her heart, and suddenly she didn't want to be alone any more.

It was well past midnight, but she didn't care. She swiftly changed into trousers and a sweater, gathered up her bag and jacket and went down to hail a taxi to take her to the hospital. If nothing else, she could have these hours with her daughter. It was little enough to ask.

Wendy welcomed her with a smile, chatting in undertones for a while before leaving Claudia alone with her sleeping child. Natalie was no longer hooked up to the monitors, and lay peacefully with a doll in her arms. Claudia bent down to brush a kiss on one satin cheek, and caught a glimpse of the gold crucifix Marco had given her. She was glad the two of them had got on. It would be good for Natalie to know Tyler wasn't all she had.

Claudia drew up a chair, and, as before, peace seemed to fall around her. The book Marco had been reading lay abandoned on the table, and she picked it up, quickly losing herself in the magic of Narnia as she had when she was not much older than Natalie. It had been an escape then, but now it was a joy, and so lost was she that it was a long while before she became aware that Natalie was no longer asleep, but lay quietly watching her.

For a moment they looked at each other, then Claudia slowly closed the book. 'You should be asleep,' she said, smiling faintly.

There was uncertainty in the wide hazel eyes. 'You were here before. You were watching me.'

'Yes, I was. I like doing it. I used to sit and watch you often when you were a baby. It made me feel that not everything was bad,' Claudia told her with simple honesty.

'If it wasn't bad why did you go?' Natalie asked with characteristic bluntness.

Claudia sighed, eyes clouding. 'Your daddy told me a lie. If he hadn't I wouldn't have left you. I don't expect you to believe that right away, but it's the truth. I love you very dearly, I always have, but I've no way of proving it.'

Small fingers picked at the doll's blonde tresses as Natalie frowned. 'Do you like Tyler?'

Claudia was glad the soft lighting hid the way her cheeks went pink. 'Yes, I do, very much.'

'So do I. I wish he was my real daddy. Daddy told lies.' There was a wealth of hurt hidden behind that blunt statement, and it brought a lump to Claudia's throat.

'I know, but you can trust Tyler,' she answered huskily.

Those penetrating eyes shot to her mother's. 'He says you want to get to know me. Does that mean you want me to go and live with you?'

Claudia realised she was in a minefield that required precision handling. 'I would like that very much, but not yet, and then only if you wanted it too,' she said gently. 'The choice will be yours.'

'Good,' Natalie said swiftly, ''cos I don't want to go.'

Swallowing the hurt, Claudia tipped her head back. 'I didn't think you would. All I want for now is a chance for us to be friends.'

'Why—because you want my money?' the little girl demanded, instantly suspicious.

Claudia sighed in irritation. 'Most certainly not. I don't need your money because I have enough of my own. So will you once and for all get that ridiculous notion out of your head?' She finished far more sharply than she'd intended, but Gordon's lie had made her so angry. Now contrite, she reached out a hand, only to draw it away swiftly in confusion. Tears burned at the back of her eyes, and she laughed bitterly. 'Look at me! I'm afraid to even touch you in case you pull away from me!' Jerkily she got to her feet and walked away to the window, calling herself all sorts of a fool.

'C-Claudia?'

The childish voice using her name had her gasping and swinging round in amazement. Natalie lifted a diffident shoulder.

'I guess... maybe... friends is OK, if you want.'

The world spun dizzily for a second or two. 'Oh, I want all right!' she exclaimed, then sobered when she saw how defensive her daughter had become. She was, after all, only a little girl who felt abandoned and who didn't know whom she could trust, including her mother. Stilling her own heart, Claudia returned to her seat and picked up the book. 'Would you like me to read to you? It would help you sleep,' she offered.

'If you like,' Natalie agreed, snuggling down.

Clearing her throat and surreptitiously wiping away a tear, Claudia found the right place and began to read.

Towards dawn Claudia collected her belongings and slipped out of the room. Natalie had fallen asleep hours ago, leaving her mother in silence, to think. A breakthrough had been made, however tentative. She wasn't about to question the how or why of it, but simply take full advantage.

Stifling a yawn, she turned towards the lifts and halted. On a chair a little way down, legs stretched out before him, hands in the trouser pockets of his dinner suit, sat Tyler. Her surprise was total. After the way he had left her she hadn't expected to see him. He hadn't changed, yet he must have been back to the hotel to discover she wasn't there. Just how long had he been sitting there, and why hadn't he come in?

Her espadrilles didn't make much noise, yet it was enough to have Tyler open his eyes and glance her way. Standing up, he waited for her to join him, taking careful stock of her pale cheeks, tired eyes and the shadows beneath them.

'This is crazy. You won't be helping Natalie if you knock yourself up,' he told her shortly.

'I'll be all right,' she protested, elbowing her way past and heading for the nearest lift.

'Sure, you look it,' his mocking rejoinder followed her.

Claudia stopped and swung on him, too tired for this. 'OK, so it's crazy. But sometimes I just have to be near her. To convince myself it isn't all a dream.'

The lift arrived and Tyler took her arm to steer her into it, punching the ground-floor button. He surveyed her with a set expression. 'It's real. How much more persuading do you need?'

'One hell of a lot. You have to lose something to truly value it.' She looked away from him, lips twisting. 'Obviously you've never lost anything of value.' Certainly he didn't put her in that category.

The lift opened and they made their way out into the beginning of another glorious day.

'The car's over here.' He indicated the car park.

Claudia allowed herself to be settled in the passenger-seat. She felt weary, but satisfied too. When Tyler joined her and set the car in motion she was silent for a while, but then couldn't resist saying, 'Did you enjoy your dinner?'

He shot her a considering look. 'Very much.'

Claudia stared out of the window. He wasn't about to give anything away, and, though a thousand questions struggled to be voiced, she held them back. 'Why did you come to collect me? Were you checking up?'

'When you weren't in bed I knew where you'd be. I thought you'd appreciate a lift back to the hotel; nothing more.'

'So dinner turned into an all-night party, did it?' she snapped, then could have bitten her tongue out when Tyler laughed.

'What has that brain of yours been conjuring up? A night of abandoned passion? Audrey would be quite flattered, I think.'

'Audrey?' she latched on to the name sharply, and felt the brush of his mocking blue gaze.

'A market analyst, whom I consult occasionally. She dined me right royally, and then we spent the next few hours locked in a passionate argument on the value of recycling waste,' he finished wryly.

Claudia's eyes were wide. 'You mean ... all night?' she asked incredulously.

He shrugged. 'Only until one o'clock. The rest of the time I spent making the acquaintance of an extremely uncomfortable hospital chair.'

She was floored by his admission. 'But ... why?' she asked helplessly.

'Because I had no idea when you would leave, and I didn't fancy the idea of you walking the streets alone in search of a taxi. There are some nasty individuals out there. Put it down as a noble gesture on my part.'

It was the very last thing she would have expected from him. 'I don't know what to say.'

'Don't say anything. Just try to curb this tendency of yours until we take Natalie home.

It will be safer, and perhaps you won't find the need,' he told her brusquely.

She didn't argue because he had raised a more important point. 'I've been meaning to ask you where you live, other than Shropshire, I mean.'

'In a beautiful valley near Church Stretton. That's a village north of Ludlow.'

'I see. Well, if Natalie's discharged next week, I'd better get on to an estate agent right away.' She'd have to get a map, too, or she'd be hopelessly lost.

'Estate agent? What the hell for?' Tyler's sharp query broke into her thoughts.

She looked up. 'To find a house, of course.'

Tyler swore, steered the car into the car park, switched off the engine and turned to her, face etched into lines of anger. 'Don't you think it would be better to *live* with Natalie for a while before swanning off?'

His assumption fanned her anger. 'I don't intend to "swan off", as you so inelegantly put it!' Claudia retorted just as fiercely. 'I have to stay somewhere. As we both know, Natalie lives in your house—for the moment—a place I'm hardly likely to be welcome!'

'Nevertheless, that's exactly where you'll stay!' Tyler informed her tersely.

Claudia's anger drifted into shock. 'But...you don't want me there!'

A nerve ticked away in his jaw. 'That's as maybe. Right now I'm thinking of Natalie. If you're ever going to achieve a relationship with your daughter, and she with you, you have to be there, Claudia. Right in the house. I may not like it, but I'll accept it. Then, if you must look for a place of your own, you can do so from there.'

It was so unexpected that Claudia floundered around in her gratitude. 'Thank you. I...um...I never expected you to be so generous. I'll try not to get in your way,' she promised huskily.

Tyler gave a harsh bark of laughter. 'Don't bother. A man would have to be blind not to know you're around, and even then I don't think it would work! Now I don't know about you, but I could do with some sleep,' he declared, climbing from the car.

Claudia did likewise, hardly knowing what to make of this new turn of events. Last night he had been furious with her. This morning he had shown concern for her health and welfare. The inconsistency kept her off balance, and yet at the same time it kept alive that faint flicker of hope. Everything pointed to a degree of caring that his remoteness belied. Yet what if she was wrong? If she dug underneath the surface would she like what she found?

She shivered a little. Was it from anticipation or alarm? She didn't know, but one way or another she was bound to find out.

CHAPTER SEVEN

SITTING back on her heels, Claudia wiped the back of her hand over her brow. The sun was scorching. She could feel the heat on her shoulders and legs where her shorts and strapless top left her skin bare. Fortunately she had skin that tanned easily, but, even so, she had taken no risks, rubbing on sunscreen before coming out to dig away at the hardened earth of the flowerbeds.

The sound of squeals and splashes from behind her drew her attention round to where Natalie, clad in a concealing swimsuit, was trying to drown Tyler in a spray of icy water. Not that it would stay icy for long in the type of weather they had been having since bringing Natalie home to White Gables.

Although she and her daughter had taken full advantage of the weather, Tyler had been shut up in his study most of the time. It had taken Natalie's persuasion to lure him out into the sunshine today to fill up the paddling pool on the lawn. Not that he showed signs of annoyance at being interrupted. On the contrary, he was throwing himself into the game with an abandon that gave Claudia equal amounts of amusement and dismay.

As she watched he caught Natalie squarely in the face with a handful of water. Laughing, he stood above her spluttering figure, hands hooked lazily on his hips.

Claudia found her eyes drinking in his sun-bronzed body, with its only covering a pair of cut-off denim shorts. The frayed edges hugged his muscled thighs and she followed the lines of his straight legs down to his bare feet. Clothed, he had stirred her senses, but stripped, he started up a deep longing which she knew would not be assuaged.

Tyler flexed his arms and drew her eyes to his wide-shouldered torso. In her mind she saw her hands run over the sleek planes of his back, her tactile exploration arousing them both. A flush rose in her cheeks and her pulse quickened in reaction. She had to clench her hands against a powerful urge to go to him.

Some of her strong emotions must have reached him through the charged air, for Tyler turned his head, his blue eyes boring into hers. Then slowly, almost as if he couldn't help himself, they lowered, passing over her glowing figure, taking in her long, shapely legs and her seductively rounded breasts which surged against the material of her top, giving

blatant evidence of the havoc his inspection
was creating. When his gaze ascended once
more to her flushed face even the distance between them couldn't hide that Tyler was not
unmoved.

They remained a tableau oblivious to the
outside world, but what might have happened
next Claudia would never know, for Natalie
demanded his attention and the tension was
broken. He turned away, and Claudia let out
her breath in a wobbly sigh. That look had
shaken her. How wrong she had been these
last few weeks. Tyler had been so cool, so
distant, that he had fooled her into thinking
he had mastered his attraction. He had treated
her to a brand of casual friendship that had
been daunting. Not by a look or word had he
shown that her presence affected him at all.
It had been disheartening, but now she knew
it had been deliberate. A near-perfect attempt
to blind her to the truth. But for that brief
exchange just now she might never have realised. The mask had slipped, and now they
both knew what he had striven to hide. The
wanting remained, a current as treacherous as
any undertow. But to whom?

If it was a weapon in her meagre armoury
why did she feel defenceless?

Claudia's self-absorption was broken by the sound of footsteps on the patio which bordered the bed she was working on. She looked up to see Wendy bearing a tray of glasses and a large pitcher of iced lemonade. The real stuff, home-made by Tyler's housekeeper, Mary Barrett.

'Mary thought you could do with this,' the young woman declared with a grin, setting the tray down on the wrought-iron patio table.

Claudia abandoned fork and gloves with a laugh. 'Oh, boy, could I! That woman is a marvel,' she added, walking round to take a seat and swallow a mouthful with a satisfied sigh.

'She's certainly a good advertisement for her own cooking,' Wendy agreed, picturing as she did so the housekeeper's well-rounded proportions.

'Hmm,' Claudia nodded, her eyes straying to where Natalie and Tyler were still playing.

'You must be pleased how well Natalie's improved,' Wendy said, following her gaze. 'You seem to be getting along so much better, too. Even Mary's told me that she can see Natalie's blossoming these days, and it isn't just because her health has improved.'

It was true, although Claudia hadn't wanted to tempt the devil by saying so. She was very much aware that it was still early days yet. Natalie hadn't totally dropped her guard, but she no longer openly rejected her mother. They had found a middle ground. Had been forced to, really, because they spent so much time together. For which Claudia knew she had Wendy to thank. The other woman had taken a deliberate back seat so that mother and daughter could be together.

Mostly that meant playing the games Natalie wanted and reading to her, but also her daughter liked to listen to tales of all her other relatives in Italy. She had a thirst for knowledge that sometimes had to be curtailed or Claudia knew she could be talking all night! But every question brought them closer. About her own father, though, Natalie rarely spoke, but the times she did the statements were very revealing. Wendy had been right. Natalie knew her father hadn't loved her—and she had no grounds for, but plenty of doubts against, believing her mother loved her.

Who could blame her? Claudia certainly didn't. It was up to her to prove it, if she could, and she would move heaven and earth to do so.

Her thoughts were distracted by Natalie, who trotted up, her eyes alight with laughter, a healthy flush on her cheeks.

'Tyler says he wants some fresh air, and he'll take me on a picnic if I can be ready in ten minutes,' she declared, hopping from foot to foot. 'I can go, can't I, Claudia? Do say yes!' She pleaded with her big eyes.

As she let her eyes drift to where Tyler stood, Claudia wondered if she would ever hear Natalie call her mother. But at least she had asked her first, and that was something. So she gave her daughter a smile.

'I don't see why not, if Wendy says you're well enough,' she qualified.

'She's fine. The outing will use up some of her energy.'

'Oh, goody!' Natalie cheered, and would have run across to Tyler only he saved her the trouble by coming to them. 'They said I can go,' she told him, hanging on his arm.

Tyler smiled down into her excited face. 'Then you'd better go and get ready, hadn't you?' he told her, and Natalie immediately headed for the house.

Wendy stood up. 'I'd better go and help her,' she excused, and went after her charge.

With the others gone Claudia was very much aware of Tyler's near-naked body so close to hers. She had to lick her lips to moisten them enough to speak, and then her voice was still husky.

'Who's providing the feast?'

He looked down at her, eyes shuttered, obviously regretting those revealing moments just now. 'We'll buy something out. Hadn't you better hurry? We won't wait for stragglers,' he said curtly.

'Me?' she asked, startled, having naturally assumed she wasn't included.

'Don't you want to come?' Tyler mocked. 'I'll understand if you have more important things to do, but I doubt Natalie will. It was her idea that you join us.' An idea that he would have liked to veto, obviously.

Claudia sat up, annoyed by his mockery. 'I'm sorry if it goes against the grain, but this was your choice. If you regret it —— '

'Whatever I feel, the arrangement stands. Natalie wants you with us. So if you don't want to disappoint her you'd better hustle,' he advised shortly.

Claudia hustled, her joy at this first overture from her daughter tempered by Tyler's reaction. He resented her for the attraction he felt, and wanted her to know it. Swiftly she showered and changed into jeans and a T-shirt, then slipped a blouse and sunglasses into a capacious straw bag along with anything else she thought might be needed. Finally, she ran a brush through her hair, slipped sandals on her feet, and hurried down to join them.

Natalie was already in the back seat of the car, and any doubts that Claudia had about where she was to sit were settled when Tyler held open the door to the front passenger-seat for her.

They drove to the lovely old town of Ludlow, where the impressive remains of the red sandstone castle, built on the orders of the Earl of Shrewsbury, perched majestically on the hill-top. To Claudia's amusement, Tyler gave in to Natalie's urgings that they visit the castle, even though he complained, with a distinct twinkle in his eye, that she had seen it a hundred times already.

She laughed at him as the little girl, dressed now in shorts and T-shirt, went ahead. 'You're putty in her hands!'

His reply showed he had slipped into a cordial mood. 'I'm not the one who's about to be dragged up every tower and down into every dungeon.'

Which proved to be all too true. Claudia had never been fond of small dark places, but she would have put up with hours in one just for the pleasure of having Natalie holding her hand. She doubted her daughter had any idea of how it made her mother feel, but she knew that the sparkle of moisture in her eye wasn't missed by Tyler. He said nothing, simply followed behind them, hands tucked casually into the pockets of his jeans.

From the castle with its lush lawns they took a walk about the town, where Tyler disappeared into a bakery emitting enticing smells, to reappear with several paper bags and a cardboard box. Claudia carried the squash bottles he purchased later on as they headed back to where they had parked the car.

This time they drove up into the green hills of the border country, and stopped to picnic on a stretch of moorland that gave them a glorious view, to the west of the mountains of Wales, and to the north-east the long ridge of Wenlock Edge. Sheep cropped their way back and forth about them as they sat on a car blanket and helped themselves to the delicious array of sandwiches Tyler had bought.

Natalie polished off an oozing jam doughnut and licked her fingers enthusiastically. 'That was great! Tyler gets all the best things! I bet you never had a picnic like this when you were little,' she told her mother with a faint air of smugness.

Claudia smiled wryly, meeting the challenge. 'I never had a picnic at all. It wasn't considered proper. My governess had strict ideas on what a well-brought-up young lady should do.'

Natalie pulled a face. 'It sounds stuffy. I thought you lived like a princess. Daddy said you lived all alone in a big house with hundreds of servants.'

Claudia was constantly surprised at what Gordon had chosen to tell their daughter. 'I did, although my cousin Amelia was there too. But I'll tell you something: I'd much rather have eaten meals like this. There's no fun sitting at the end of a long table, with servants waiting to clear your used dishes away, but who never speak to you.' Her eyes wandered away to Tyler, to see how he responded to all this, but he was lying back, eyes closed. She couldn't even tell if he was listening.

'Didn't you have any fun?' Natalie wanted to know next.

Claudia ran a mental eye over her childhood and youth. It would be easy to elicit sympathy but she didn't want to make herself out to be a martyr. 'Not fun as you mean it. My fun was books. I read everything I could lay my hands on.' She laughed at the memory.

'That's when I really thought I was a princess. Waiting for a knight to come and carry me off on a white horse.'

'Someone like Daddy?' Natalie put in slyly, making her mother draw in her breath sharply.

'Yes, I really thought he was. He was so handsome and charming, and said everything I wanted to hear.' Even now her own naïveté hurt. But she had been young and alienated—and utterly beguiled by him.

Natalie fell silent, her fingers picking away at the short grass. When she did speak there was such a wealth of bleakness in her seven-year-old voice, hidden behind an almost adult casualness, that Claudia was torn apart.

'Daddy said he loved me, but I knew he didn't. He used to show me off to the ladies he brought home, but he never bothered when we were alone. I heard him talking on the telephone once. He said he'd never wanted children. That I was a mistake. And the worst thing was that I looked like you.'

The hand Claudia reached out to rest on her daughter's dark hair trembled visibly. 'Darling, you're the best mistake he ever made. But *I* wanted you. I never regretted having you, not for a single second. And I'm proud that you look like me.'

Natalie looked up, her eyes filled with doubt and confusion. 'I've got freckles,' she pointed out doggedly.

'I love freckles,' Claudia declared huskily.

Her daughter's chin wobbled disastrously, then she swiftly bent and picked up the remains of a roll. 'I'm going to feed the sheep,' she said, jumping up and hurrying away.

'Don't go far!' Claudia called out after her, biting her lip as she watched the proud little back recede.

'She'll be all right.'

Tyler's comment brought Claudia's head round. So he had been listening after all. 'I hope so.'

'She just needs time to think,' he added, sitting up. 'You sounded as if you knew how Gordon felt about Natalie.'

'Wendy told me,' she admitted.

'Wendy?'

Claudia nodded. 'She's a very astute woman. She also turned Gordon down when he tried it on with her.'

Tyler dragged a hand through his hair. 'God, you make me feel as if I've been living in another world!'

'The main thing is that you made Natalie happy. Gave her a sense of worth. The other day she told me she wished you were her real father. There's no greater accolade than that, Tyler.'

He gave her an odd look. 'Was it true what you told her, that you and your cousin lived alone?'

'Basically. Our great-uncles were our guardians. They had us raised in a style that befitted our position in life.' Claudia smiled wryly and shrugged. 'Oh, they were kind enough, but they had no idea how stifling such a regime was. To me at least.'

'Your cousin didn't feel the same?'

'She didn't have Latin blood in her veins.' Claudia laughed.

'You didn't go to college?' he probed, watching the play of emotion over her face.

Now she could joke about it. 'I went to a very proper ladies' academy. It fitted me for everything but the real world. I was ready to rebel when I met Gordon. The uncles fought hard to make me change my mind, but I was eighteen by then and they couldn't stop me. Too late I discovered they were right.' There was no inflexion in her voice. She had done all her regretting years ago. 'I told you he was never faithful, but he knew my weakness only too well. I had too much pride to run home.' Instead she had stayed and put up with all the slights, the humiliations. Until she hadn't been able to take any more.

Tyler tipped his head forward the better able to survey her profile. 'Yet you were in Italy on your own.'

'I was alone because I needed to think. Gordon had other fish to fry here in England. Angie, I think her name was.' Glancing sideways, she caught his frown and smiled. 'Gordon never kept that sort of thing to himself. Anyway, I no longer cared because I'd decided to divorce him.'

Tyler frowned. 'You're saying you'd already decided to leave him when you met me?' he verified.

'I simply couldn't take any more.'

There was an expression on Tyler's face that defied description. 'If you'd already decided to leave him why the hell did you go back? Surely you hadn't expected him to have changed?' he demanded angrily.

Claudia let her gaze drift to Natalie. 'I didn't go back to him, not the way you mean. At least, not then.'

'You sure as hell didn't divorce him either!'

She glared at him. 'I intended to. If I couldn't have you I certainly didn't want him! But when I got back Gordon was different. He caught me at a vulnerable moment and, like an idiot, I fell for his lies. By the time I realised what he was up to Natalie was on the way. So I stayed, and Gordon reverted to his old ways.

'I lost track of all his women; but for Natalie I would probably have turned a blind eye if he hadn't decided he wanted me. I refused. I forgot that nobody said no to Gordon,' she said bitterly.

'For God's sake!' Tyler exploded.

Claudia grimaced. 'I left the next day—and you know what happened.'

Tyler sank back on his heels, the colour draining out of him visibly. 'God!' He turned his head away, watching, without seeing, Natalie coming back. After a long while he said, 'You should never have gone back.'

Claudia couldn't believe her ears. 'I don't believe this! You're not making any sense, Tyler. According to you, I was wrong to leave Gordon, but wrong to go back! What was I supposed to do—appeal to you for help? But you'd already made your judgement and turned your back on me. For you, I didn't exist. You were never an option, were you? I made my decisions as best I could. When are you going to make yours? When are you going to decide what you do mean and what you do want?'

'Are you two fighting?'

Natalie's question drew their startled attention, neither having heard her approach. While Claudia froze, wondering just what her daughter might have overheard, Tyler recovered fast.

'Not on a day like today, pumpkin. We were just talking over old times.' Smiling, he pulled her on to his knee. 'Well, how did you get on? Have you still got two hands?'

'They kept running away,' Natalie related in disgust, and the moment passed.

Claudia gathered together their rubbish, listening to them talk with half an ear. She knew neither of them had forgotten what had been said. She didn't know quite what to make of Tyler's ambivalent reaction. Should she be encouraged that it hadn't been as rigid as before? But did that really mean he had softened in any way? These were things she really needed to know, because Nancy was due in Manchester any day now, expecting to hear from her. So much depended on the climate being right. Yet perhaps she had made Tyler think, and that could only be to the good, couldn't it?

Fingers snapped before her eyes, making her blink and focus on the man and girl. They had an arm around each other, and looked so

happy and at ease that Claudia's heart contracted sharply.

'Sorry, I was miles away,' she apologised,
forcing a smile to her lips.

'We're going to play frisbee. Are you
coming?' Natalie wanted to know. When her
mother nodded she jumped to her feet. Tyler
rose nimbly and offered Claudia a hand up.

She accepted it, but once on her feet he
didn't immediately let her go. The action
brought her eyes to his face.

'What do you want from me, Claudia?' His
voice was low, for her ears only.

The answer was absurdly simple, yet impossible to utter. 'You must decide that for
yourself, Tyler,' she told him huskily, and,
withdrawing her hands, she went past him to
her daughter.

For a moment Tyler watched them in silence, his face sombre, thoughts far from
pleasant. Then Natalie beckoned and he
forced a smile to his lips and went to join
them.

Claudia indicated left and steered the white
Metro into the narrow road that led up into
the valley and the house. She had scarcely
spoken to Tyler since their picnic yesterday.
He had shut himself into his study and not

emerged, even for meals. The housekeeper reported that he scarcely touched what she took him either; he just sat at his desk, staring out of the window.

Claudia kept her thoughts to herself. It would be easy to jump to conclusions. To read more into the situation. Her caution had proved to be wise. When she had sought him out to ask him to look after Natalie while she went shopping in Church Stretton he had been short to the point of brusqueness.

He had agreed to look after Natalie, though. Which hadn't surprised her, for he always had time for the young girl. It was Wendy's day off, and Mary had needed to go and see her sister, who had had a nasty fall only that morning and been taken to hospital.

Not that Claudia minded the trip. It had given her the opportunity to phone Nancy Wheeler's hotel without danger of being overheard. The only snag had been that the older woman had been out, and she had been obliged to leave a message giving the telephone number of the house. It certainly wasn't an ideal arrangement, but the only one she could think of.

She turned a corner and White Gables came into view. It was a sight that never failed to please her. Set at the base of a hill, the house was surrounded at a distance on three sides by the woods. The gently sloping lawn led down to the lane, set with flowerbeds and a fish-pond. On the other side of the lane, two fields opened up with the faint glint of a stream at the bottom of them.

The house itself was old, a cross between a large farmhouse and a small manor, but it had a charm and beauty that made her wish she had the ability to capture it on canvas. Built from mellow stone, with roses trained up the walls, the whole front seemed taken over by windows, just now thrust open to the summer breezes that set the sparkling white nets billowing out.

Parking the car, Claudia collected the box of groceries from the back and carried them round to the kitchen. She felt uncomfortably hot and sticky, despite her lemon cotton sundress, and she thought longingly of the swimming pool at Aunt Lucia's villa.

The house had that peculiar echo of emptiness, but she called out anyway, unsurprised to be answered by silence. They couldn't have gone far, because she had caught sight of Tyler's car in the garage. She knew a moment's disappointment, for she would have enjoyed a walk herself, then shrugged it off and began putting things away.

By the time she had finished Claudia was gasping for a drink, something long and cool. She walked through to the lounge. The cocktail cabinet was a cupboard that swivelled, and, unable to find what she wanted on one side, she automatically turned to the other. But instead of finding more bottles she saw that the shelves were filled with videotapes. Even then she would have turned away if Natalie's name hadn't caught her eye, and she bent forward for a closer inspection. They were nearly all of her daughter, according to the inscriptions, and all at varying stages in her young life.

The video and television were near by, and Claudia didn't hesitate, taking the earliest film and slotting it in, then sitting on her knees with a racing heart, waiting for the picture to come up on the screen. When it did the surge of emotion stopped her heart. These were the growing years that she had missed. Mostly it was Wendy playing with the tiny Natalie. There were glimpses of Gordon, but never of Tyler. So he must be holding the camera, wielding it with a love that was apparent to Claudia as she watched her daughter running and laughing, hearing the never before heard sounds of Natalie's attempts to speak.

She watched, hand pressed over trembling lips to stifle her sobs as tears streamed down her cheeks. Laughing brokenly at antics she would never see first-hand. As each film was discarded for the next the tightness in her chest grew, and she was unaware that her body rocked backwards and forwards in a vain attempt to ease the pain. There were moments when it seemed unbearable, yet she couldn't look away, for this was the only way she had of filling the void of those empty years.

She was insensible to everything else about her. She didn't hear the voices outside or the tiny gasp as two figures came to a halt in the doorway, watching her. She didn't see a pale-cheeked Natalie cross the room to kneel beside her, a deep frown creasing her smooth brow.

'Mamma, what's wrong?'

That alone penetrated, and Claudia turned, drawing in a ragged, painful breath. 'What?' She doubted her sanity. Had she really heard that?

Natalie blinked, her large eyes starting to shine as her chin wobbled. 'Why are you crying, Mamma?'

Claudia couldn't have answered; all she could do was sweep her daughter into her arms and hold her crushingly tight. She wasn't mad; she had heard it. Natalie had called her 'Mamma'. And, wonder of wonders, a pair of small arms crept up around her neck.

'Don't cry, Mamma, don't cry!'' Natalie's words were drowned in her own tears.

Claudia closed her eyes. 'I won't. Just hold me. Hold me and never let go, because I love you so very much. So very, very much.'

How long they stayed like that she never did know, but the tears dried and her leg went to sleep. So she moved at last, switching off the machines before moving to the couch, keeping Natalie in the shelter of her arm.

'Why were you crying?' Natalie didn't remain quiet for long.

Claudia used one hand to brush the hair out of her daughter's eyes. 'Because the films reminded me of all I had missed. I'd wanted so much to share all that, and I could have done, except that I thought you were dead.'

Natalie's head came up sharply but her eyes showed no surprise. 'Did Daddy tell you that?'

Her daughter's perception amazed her, so that she could only nod, then add, 'I'm sorry,' although she wasn't sure exactly what she was apologising for.

Even so, Natalie seemed to understand, for she sighed. 'Daddy always told lies. Tyler doesn't,' she added slyly.

Claudia smiled faintly. 'No, and neither do I. I meant it when I said I love you.'

'Does that mean you're going to stay?'

'I want to, but it probably won't be here. This is Tyler's home, you know. I'll have to look for a house near by. Then you can come and live with me, but still be near Tyler.'

Natalie gave that some thought. 'You could stay here if you married Tyler,' she said guilelessly, and her mother jumped.

'Yes,' she said with an odd laugh, 'but people don't marry each other for those reasons,' she pointed out.

'Don't you love him, then?' Natalie asked next, sitting up and looking her mother squarely in the eye.

Claudia had never faced such direct questions from one so young. For a moment she was all at sea, but then she decided that honesty was best. 'Yes, I do love him.'

'Well, then?'

Claudia had to laugh. 'Oh, Natalie, it isn't that simple. Don't try matchmaking, because you'll only be disappointed.'

Natalie looked about to argue, then thought better of it. 'OK,' she said easily, which gave her mother a moment of doubt, until she banished it with a smile. 'Tyler took me for a walk by the stream and I picked some flowers. Will you help me stick them in my book?'

'Go and get it, then, while I make myself some coffee. We'll sit outside, hmm?'

'OK.' Natalie grinned and hurried off.

Claudia smiled after her. Still in a state of bemusement, she quickly tidied up the films and headed for the kitchen. To her surprise she discovered Tyler there, and he must have heard her coming for he already had the coffee made. He poured a cup and pushed it across the table to her.

'I think you need that right about now,' he said, picking up his own cup and watching her over the top of it.

'Thanks.' Claudia sat down and sipped gratefully.

'So, Natalie has finally been won over,' Tyler observed drily, causing her to look up with a frown.

'Do you mind?'

Tyler shrugged and set his cup aside, crossing his arms on the table. 'I don't have the right. She's your daughter.'

Claudia lowered her cup slowly. 'Why do I get the feeling there's a ''but'' there somewhere? I thought you wanted me to succeed, or was it all just talk?'

'No, it wasn't just talk,' Tyler returned swiftly. 'I am pleased for you, but you can believe that or not as you like.'

'So what's the "but"?'

Tyler glanced down at his cup. 'I don't want to lose touch with Natalie completely.'

'I wouldn't do that to you, Tyler,' Claudia reassured instantly. 'I know what Natalie means to you, and you to her. I've already told her I intend to find a house near by,' she informed him steadily.

'And what did she say to that?'

Claudia couldn't hide her grin as she studied her cooling coffee. 'She wants me to stay here. Her solution to the obvious difficulties is that we should get married,' she said blandly. Of course, she had to look up then, to witness his reaction. His amusement was vaguely shocking when she had rather expected to be harangued for putting her daughter up to it.

'Did she indeed, the little minx?' he said with a laugh.

'Naturally, I told her that was unlikely,' Claudia felt bound to say.

Tyler's eyes narrowed. 'And she accepted that?' At her nod, he grimaced. 'Hmm, that means she's up to something. There's a hell of a lot of truth in the old adage that when kids go quiet that's the time to start worrying. And we both know what Natalie's like!'

Claudia dropped her lashes hastily. 'You may, but I don't,' she said huskily.

There was a short silence, then Tyler sighed. 'I'm sorry, Claudia, that was crass of me.'

She raised a diffident shoulder. 'It doesn't matter. Besides, what I don't know I intend to find out,' she finished positively.

Tyler looked grimly amused. 'I'm sure you will. I can see where Natalie gets her determination from,' he declared as he pushed himself to his feet. 'By the way, did you bring something dressy with you?'

Claudia blinked up at him. 'Why...yes, but...'

'Good, wear it tonight. I'm taking you out to dinner.'

'Dinner?' she exclaimed, surprised, not to say stunned.

Tyler's lips curved mockingly. 'It's a wonder to see you lost for words for once. Just be ready at eight, Claudia. You've had little cause for celebration lately, and I don't intend to be accused of letting you miss out on this one. Any objections?'

Claudia had the feeling her expression resembled that of a fish out of water. Hastily she composed herself. 'No, none. Thank you, Tyler. I didn't expect it.'

There was a hint of softness in his blue eyes. 'I know. You've got used to not expecting things, haven't you?'

Soft colour washed into her cheeks. 'I don't want your pity, Tyler. I haven't asked for it,' she repudiated swiftly.

A look crossed his face that she couldn't interpret. 'This isn't pity, Claudia—far from it,' he replied enigmatically, and left before she could ask what it was.

Remaining at the table, Claudia didn't know what to think. There was danger in reading too much into the invitation, and yet her heart had accelerated crazily. It still hadn't settled down, though she resolutely battened down her wanton thoughts. He was just being kind, nothing more. But what if...?

With a groan she finished off her coffee. Lord, she was acting like a teenager instead of a woman with a seven-year-old daughter. Who, if she wasn't mistaken, was coming to find her. Reluctantly pushing all thoughts of the evening ahead from her mind, she went to join her.

CHAPTER EIGHT

CLAUDIA scraped up the last crumbs of strawberry gâteau and popped them in her mouth with a sigh. The meal had been excellent from start to finish, but the company... Tyler had been in a strange mood, quiet and preoccupied. From the moment they had left Natalie in Wendy's care he had been subdued, as if there was something weighing heavily on his mind.

Laying down her fork, she looked across at him. In his dark dinner suit and dazzling white shirt he was quite devastatingly attractive tonight, as every one of her senses registered constantly. 'That was delicious.' Her voice got his attention, but his smile was brief and clearly an effort.

'You always did enjoy your food. It's a pleasure to escort a woman who doesn't pick at her meal. I remember thinking you had an ongoing love-affair with pasta.'

Claudia laughed, though there had been a time when she couldn't see pasta without painful memories. 'I still do. It must be the

218

Latin in me,' she joked, reaching for her cup
of coffee. 'I'm surprised you remember.'

Tyler's lips curved wryly. 'I've been re-
membering a lot of things lately. Things
that...' He hesitated and Claudia stepped in
quickly.

'You'd hoped you'd forgotten?' she said
flippantly, only to be brought up short by the
impatience in his face.

'Things that meant nothing at the time, but
which take on new meaning in the light of
what you've told me,' he contradicted.

'I didn't think you were listening,' she re-
joined tartly.

Tyler laughed. 'Believe me, you have impressive ways of making yourself heard,' he
observed drily.

Soft colour washed into her cheeks and she
cleared her throat. 'I just wanted you to understand. I wasn't making demands or
expecting anything more from you.'

Idly he stirred his own coffee. 'Weren't
you? Aren't you being a little less than honest
with yourself, Claudia?' he asked softly, and
her nerves jolted.

Her eyes widened as she met his, 'I don't
know what you mean,' she denied.

A smile curved his lips. 'Don't act dumb,
Claudia; we both know you're far from being

that. Weren't you really hoping we'd get together again?'

She frowned, not knowing where the conversation was leading. 'That *would* be rather dumb of me, wouldn't it?' she drawled with heavy sarcasm.

Tyler looked sceptical. 'You mean it's never crossed your mind?' he probed.

His persistence touched a raw nerve. 'I'm only human, you know!' she snapped. 'Of course it's crossed my mind. But don't flatter yourself it was more than that.'

'That's a pity; I was rather hoping it was.'

Claudia stared at him, totally dumbfounded. This she hadn't expected. 'For weeks now you've been telling me I was beyond the pale. Are you saying you've changed your mind?'

Tyler took a deep breath. 'Hard as it may be to believe, yes, I have. I had no right to condemn you for wanting to end a marriage that was a travesty,' he said quietly.

She had waited for this, so why did she feel so anticlimactic? 'No, you didn't,' she returned baldly, waiting.

He nodded, accepting the rebuke. 'I had my reasons, which seemed good at the time. You've proved to me I was wrong.'

'Do you expect me to thank you?' she enquired levelly. What did he want of her?

Tyler shook his head. 'Do you really think I'm that much of an egotist? I admitted I was wrong because you deserved to hear it. I *expect* nothing. I *hoped* that we could put the past behind us and start afresh. The choice is yours, and I'll abide by your decision.'

Claudia dropped her gaze. Did he think it was that easy? That she'd agree just like that? She was human enough to want to turn the screw a little. 'You mean...as friends?' she probed and heard his moment of hesitation with grim satisfaction. Friendship my eye!

'If that's what you want, yes,' he agreed.

It did her heart good to hear that gritty tone in his voice. She couldn't curb the urge to squeeze a drop more blood. 'I don't know. This is all very sudden —— ' The sentence ended abruptly as his hand came across to close over hers, and she looked up at once to be caught by the glitter in his eyes.

'Damn it, Claudia, it's not sudden at all and you know it! By all means take your pound of flesh, but don't forget that we both know the spark between us is as strong now as it ever was!'

Her nerves leapt wildly in response both to his touch and his words. What he said was true, but if he expected her to leap into his arms simply because he had relented he was mistaken. She wasn't a convenience. She loved him, and as yet he had made no mention of what he felt—beside wanting her, that was.

Though her nerves were rioting, she forced herself to remain cool. 'That's beside the point, Tyler. You're going too fast. Last week you hated me——'

Again he interrupted her. 'Never!' he declared sharply, then added in a far softer tone, 'Never hated, Claudia, though I tried damn hard to.'

'You gave a good impression of despising me.'

His laughter mocked himself. 'It was myself I was despising! For what I saw as my weakness over you. You floored me when you asked me to decide what it was I wanted. I thought I knew. Yet, when I'd cooled down enough to think, I realised that what I really wanted was you. Everything else simply wasn't important.'

His confession threw Claudia into a quandary. He sounded sincere and her instinct was to agree. But he made her feel like an itch he couldn't scratch. What did he really feel? Wasn't it all too convenient?

Her doubts must have been conveyed to him, because his hand tightened on hers. 'I know; it's too fast. I haven't given you much reason to trust me. But I'm not about to rush you, Claudia. We both need to take our time.'

With what aim in mind? Getting her into his bed? That would be simple if he really tried, because she was susceptible, and they both knew it. But what about commitment? Could she trust him this time? Yet he said she could set the pace. This was no time to be faint-hearted. She could afford to agree on those terms, couldn't she?

'All right,' she agreed, her voice low and husky, and was surprised to see a flicker of relief on his face. He hadn't been certain at all that she would agree, and that very vulnerability gave her confidence a boost.

He smiled. 'Thank you. This time you won't regret it.'

She sincerely hoped not.

'There's dancing here—do you want to go down?' Tyler asked as he caught the eye of the waiter and called for the bill.

With her emotions too keyed up to go home yet, Claudia was content to prolong the evening. 'Mmm, I'd like that,' she declared with a faint smile.

Returning her smile with a warm one of his own, Tyler settled the bill and took her arm to lead her downstairs to the night-club. There were plenty of people there already, sitting or dancing, and all the tables were taken, so Tyler slipped Claudia's small silver bag into his pocket and led her on to the dance-floor, drawing her into his arms in one fluid movement.

To Claudia, as his arms closed about her, it was like coming home. She hadn't realised how lonely she had felt until the right arms held her once more. Doubts fled. The music was romantic and slow, allowing them to move together and enjoy the close contact of their bodies. Succumbing to the mood, she slipped both arms sinuously about Tyler's neck, running a sleek hand into the silky mane of hair, and let her head dip to rest against his shoulder.

She sighed, breathing in the tangy aroma of aftershave and the male scent that was Tyler's alone. How she had missed this, re-alising that subconsciously she had been waiting for a moment like this all evening. She could feel Tyler's breath warm on her neck, and then his hands were moving, gliding sen-suously up and down the line of her spine, until finally they locked together in the small of her back, holding her firmly to him so that she was heart-stoppingly aware of his desire for her.

Tyler lowered his head into the tender skin of her neck, his lips teasing their way up to her ear with delicious, spine-tingling chills. 'God, I want to kiss you so badly,' he groaned out thickly. 'Let's get out of here.' He barely waited for her agreement, simply taking her hand and pulling her after him off the dance-floor and from the building.

The night was moonless, shrouding the almost deserted car park in deep shadows. Briskly Tyler walked her with a determined stride to where he had parked the car, but instead of unlocking the doors he leant against the side and drew her towards him. Legs braced apart for support, he held her between them as his arms locked about her waist and he lowered his head. Claudia uttered a muffled, half-hearted protest before her arms slid around his neck as she lifted her head to meet the force of his kiss.

Time lost all meaning as they came together. Exchanging passion feverishly, caught up in a rip-tide of need. The kiss deepened, became an erotic voyage of rediscovery, seeking and locking in urgent response.

Lost to the world, Claudia moaned low in her throat, moving restlessly against his hard body. She wanted this quite desperately. Needed to feel again his strength enfolding her. At a time of so much uncertainty this alone was real. And Tyler felt the same. As he dragged his mouth from hers to bury it in her hair his heart raced wildly.

'I shouldn't have done that! Lord knows, I knew I wouldn't want to stop. But a car park is hardly the place for this,' he murmured huskily.

Eyes closed, battling her own senses, Claudia could only agree. 'Let's go home,' she whispered, easing herself away, not bothering to hide what her eyes revealed, knowing they mirrored the desire in his own.

The homeward journey seemed to take forever to Claudia's impatient senses, yet when they drew up before the house it was only a little after ten-thirty. The building was in darkness, save for the dimmed glow of a light behind the curtains of Natalie's room, and a slightly brighter one in the hall. Indoors, all was silent; everyone had retired to bed long ago.

Claudia could hear her heart beating loudly in the silence as she followed Tyler into the lounge. He used the dimmer switch to leave only a subdued glow from the lamps, then discarded jacket and tie before turning to where she had stopped by the couch. He came to her then, hands cupping her cheeks, tilting her face so that the light revealed the flush of desire on her skin and the bruised pink of passion-violated lips.

He seemed to have difficulty swallowing. 'Am I going too fast for you?' he whispered thickly, giving her the choice to back off if she wanted.

She knew she ought to say yes, but she just couldn't. 'No.'

His response was to sweep her up in his powerful arms and carry her effortlessly to the couch. Laying her along its cushioned length, Tyler paused only to slip off his shirt before coming down to join her. The night air was still warm after the heat of the day, and his skin held a golden sheen. Claudia could never agree with those who said the male body was not beautiful, for to her it was. The sheer texture and planes of light and shadow drew her hands like a magnet. Her eyes followed the wandering tactile investigation. She had mentally abandoned all restraint and now her passionate nature had full rein. Her concentration on the pleasure this gave her was total. Under her hands, Tyler moaned and shuddered his pleasure, but he made no move to halt her.

Propped on his side, with one large hand resting on her hip, he watched her lose herself in the sheer voluptuousness of her movements. He closed his eyes on a groan. 'God, how I've wanted you to touch me all evening. That's incredible—don't stop!'

But his very words halted her and drew her eyes up to his face. Her stillness registered slowly, opening his eyes, their gazes locked in unspoken message.

'I know, Claudia,' he whispered gruffly, and she closed her eyes as, with infinite care, he removed the fitted jacket of her suit, revealing a silky camisole top that fastened down the front with tiny buttons.

Claudia's thought processes disintegrated completely. She felt so hot with Tyler's eyes upon her, and when his hands settled on her hips and began to glide upwards so slowly, drawing her breath from her in laboured gasps, she knew he did indeed know what she wanted. She could feel her breasts swelling and hardening in anticipation of his touch. Dear lord, he was going so slowly that she felt she would go out of her mind if his hands did not soon find the resting place she desired. A small whimper caught in her throat as his fingers began to climb the lower slopes of her breasts—and then they had conquered them, rubbing and kneading, teasing her aching nipples into tight buds that surged against their flimsy covering into the palms of his hands.

'Tyler!' His name broke from her in a broken sigh, and at last she opened her eyes again to watch as he concentrated on her as she had done on him. His dark head lifted and their burning gazes met in understanding.

'God, how I've missed you, Claudia,' he declared unevenly, sliding down half over her, his arms holding her close and one trouser-clad leg thrust between hers. His mouth closed on hers again, moving urgently, and she opened her lips to his, meeting him more than halfway, drowning in kisses that left her breathless and longing for so much more.

So lost were they in each other that they didn't at first hear the ringing of the telephone, and it was quite some time before the strident insistence forced them apart.

'No,' Tyler groaned in disbelief.

'You'd better answer it before the whole house wakes up,' Claudia said practically, though it was hard to bring her scattered wits under control.

Still muttering, Tyler crossed to the unit that held the offending instrument and snatched the receiver from its rest. Claudia struggled to sit up as he barked into the mouthpiece, her sultry gaze running over his back.

Tyler turned and held out the receiver in her direction. 'It's for you.'

Her eyebrows lifted in surprise. 'For me? Are you sure?' Quickly she rose to her feet and padded over the carpet to his side, made aware, by the burning glow in his eyes, of just what an alluring picture she made. Taking the receiver from him, she jumped as his arms slid about her waist, drawing her back against him, his mouth buried against her neck.

It made her, 'Hello, who is this?' very breathless.

'Claudia? Hello, my dear, this is Nancy Wheeler,' the well-remembered soft voice introduced herself. 'I'm sorry to call so late. Was that Tyler who answered?' Nancy's voice had a slight break in it.

Claudia, who had gone rigid in alarm, softened immediately. 'Yes, it was. Are you all right?' she said with some concern, because it must have come as a shock.

'I'm fine, dear; just a little shaken at hearing his voice after all these years. He

sounded put out. Did I interrupt something?'
There was a teasing note in her voice that
didn't entirely hide the fact that she was still
quite overcome.

The question left Claudia feeling a little
hysterical herself, for here she was with Tyler
nuzzling one ear, while his mother spoke in
the other. 'Nothing...nothing important,' she
said for the benefit of both. Tyler's reaction
was to nip her lobe with his teeth.

'Tell whoever it is to ring again tomorrow,'
he advised in a whisper.

Gasping, Claudia slapped at the hands that
were wandering too freely. 'Stop it!' she
snapped, then, realising that Nancy could
hear everything, quickly covered the mouthpiece. 'For heaven's sake, Tyler, behave!' In
response, his hold relaxed fractionally and she
used the moment to slip neatly free. Backing
away, she held up a hand to ward him off.

'Please, Tyler, this is important. Why don't
you...go and make us some coffee?' she suggested hastily.

Tyler halted his advance, hands going to
hook on to his hips. 'Want to get rid of me,
hmm? Who are you talking to?' he asked
suspiciously.

'Just a friend, but it is private. Give me five
minutes, please,' she urged.

Raking a hand through his hair, he sighed. 'OK, five minutes,' he agreed and left with a warning backward look.

Sighing with relief, she took her hand away from the receiver. 'I'm sorry about that, Nancy. You got my message?'

'Yes, dear, that's why I'm ringing so late. We've had to rearrange our schedule slightly. I know it's very short notice, but we'll be coming tomorrow afternoon.'

'Tomorrow?' Claudia sank on to the nearest seat. 'I see.'

Nancy sighed. 'I know, you probably think it's too soon. Frankly, I doubt my welcome will be warm whenever I come. However, I have little choice now; tomorrow it must be.'

Hastily Claudia gathered her thoughts together. 'Actually, it might not be such a bad time to pick. Tyler has...softened a little lately. I truly believe your words might not fall on deaf ears this time.'

'Then it's agreed. All I need from you are directions; the rest is up to me, my dear,' Nancy declared purposefully.

Realising she had had a good five minutes already, Claudia quickly gave the necessary directions and rang off. Her eyes fell on her jacket lying by the couch and she picked it up, slipping it on over skin that felt a little chilled.

All desire to carry on their lovemaking had left her now in the face of Nancy's imminent visit. Tomorrow was going to be traumatic— she felt it in her bones. And what Tyler would make of her part in things she didn't care to think about!

Also, the timely interruption had given her the chance to think. Had the telephone not rung there was only one way the evening would have ended. She knew she wouldn't have regretted it, yet she had to recognise that Tyler had made no commitment. There had been no mention of love and need, only want. The very things she wanted. In the circumstances, this was much too fast.

She was buttoning her jacket when Tyler walked in mere seconds later. He faltered a moment when he saw she was dressed again, the smile fading from his lips. Still, he bore the tray to the coffee-table and offered her one of the two mugs it contained. When she took it he raised the other and eyed her over it.

'Just cold, or have you changed your mind?' he asked coolly.

Claudia cradled the mug in her hands and felt the colour rise in her cheeks. 'Both, actually. I'm sorry.'

His lips curved faintly. 'Don't be. I told you you could set the pace, that I wouldn't rush you. I thought…' He broke off and shrugged. 'I guess I was going too fast after all,' he finished wryly.

Claudia took a step towards him. 'It wasn't that I didn't want to,' she said quickly, and watched his lips twist mockingly.

'But you had second thoughts,' Tyler concluded drily. 'You don't know if you can really trust me, do you? I don't blame you. I haven't given you much reason to.'

Claudia scarcely knew whether to be glad or sorry that he had made that assumption, yet she went along with it, even though it was only partly true.

'I just need time to take it all in,' she said helplessly.

This time his smile was broader. 'And you can have it. What's one more cold shower after all the others I've had since we met again?' he teased, not without a rueful honesty.

Biting her lip, eyes revealing her remorse, Claudia set the mug down again, its contents untouched. 'I'm truly sorry, Tyler.' Stifling a yawn, she smiled crookedly. 'It's been a busy day. If you don't mind I'm going to go to bed now.'

Tyler put his mug down and came to her, catching her by the shoulders, holding her

lightly while he dropped a kiss on her brow.
'Goodnight, Claudia; sweet dreams, my love,'
he murmured, then, turning her, gave her a
gentle shove towards the door.

Bemused, she went, wondering if she had
dreamt his calling her 'my love', yet knowing
she hadn't. It was the first time he had called
her that in eight years, and it brought a lump
of emotion to her throat. As she climbed the
stairs she prayed that he meant it, that it
wasn't just words.

And that the events of the morrow wouldn't
make him regret what he had said today.

It was so quiet that Claudia could hear the
bees buzzing in the flowerbeds. Not a breath
of wind stirred the leaves on the trees, and the
heat was enervating. Lunch had been over an
hour ago now, and Tyler, who had emerged
from his study, had decided to play hookey,
and now lay dozing in a hammock.

She could see him from where she sat in the
shade of a large copper beech. Bare-chested,
one denim-clad leg dangling over the side,
foot trailing the ground, and one arm lying
across his eyes. Her vantage point had been
chosen because it gave her an uninterrupted
view of the road, down which, some time
soon, a car would appear.

The slightest movement would catch her attention, as it did now in the furthest field. Two colourful dots pin-pointed Natalie and Wendy down by the stream. Natalie had wanted her to join them, but Claudia couldn't take the risk of not being here when Nancy arrived.

Sighing, Claudia closed the book she had only been pretending to read, a frown creasing her brow. She had scarcely spoken to Tyler at lunch, and he had shut himself away long before she had risen that morning. Somehow she had expected him to seek her out after what had happened last night. Yet, though he had been friendly enough, there had been nothing special in his behaviour. It was almost as if nothing had happened yesterday. She supposed it was his way of confirming his promise not to rush her, but, contrarily, she felt let down.

A new noise reached her, and her head came up. Her eye lighted instantly on a moving blue dot, and her heart leapt as she realised it was a car. The road was used so infrequently that she knew it had to be his mother, and it meant the moment she had been waiting for had arrived. From now on there was no turning back.

The engine noise grew louder, and out of the corner of her eye Claudia saw Tyler sit up, shading his eyes against the sun's glare as he tried to make out who it was. In that moment she would have given anything to be elsewhere, and so avoid the confrontation she had been instrumental in bringing about. But it was too late to do more than cross her fingers and hope.

As the car halted at the side of the road Claudia rose and walked over to Tyler's side, knowing it would only be a matter of minutes before he recognised who their visitors were, and she had to prevent him from disappearing before a word had been exchanged. Although he didn't glance at her, he acknowledged her presence by saying, 'Who the devil can that be? I wasn't expecting anyone, were you?'

Claudia thought it wisest to let that pass. Meanwhile, Nancy and her husband had left the car and were climbing the path. A second later the tension emanating from the man beside her was palpable, and she braced herself for the storm to come.

'My God, it can't be! How the hell did she —?' The question was cut off as the truth hit him and he turned an angry, incredulous face to her. 'You! You planned this!'

Tyler exploded to his feet and Claudia grabbed hold of his arm desperately, her side vision revealing that Nancy and Oscar were now crossing the lawn.

'Just talk to her, Tyler, please. That's all she wants. You owe her that much,' she pleaded urgently.

The look he gave her could have split rocks. 'I owe her nothing!'

Angry frustration filled her. 'All right, then, you owe it to yourself!'

Blue eyes flashed warningly. 'Do I? Damn you, Claudia! You had no right to do this. Don't expect me to thank you. This time you've gone too damn far!'

Claudia didn't dare let herself think of that right now; instead she kept a firm grip on his arm and turned to greet their visitors. Nancy looked quite charming in a chiffon dress of a shade of blue much favoured by the Queen Mother, but there was a tension about her lips and eyes that belied her smile. Claudia guessed that the arm she had linked with Oscar's blazer-clad one was for moral rather than physical support. As they halted a yard away he patted her hand reassuringly.

It was Oscar who broke the silence that fell as mother and son confronted each other for the first time in twenty-odd years. 'You must be Claudia. Nancy's told me so much about you. I'm pleased to meet you at last.' He smiled warmly and held out his hand.

She shook it, gaining comfort from the gentle pressure. 'I've long admired your playing, Mr Wheeler.'

'Make it Oscar, my dear. I'm always happy to meet a fan,' he invited, then turned smoothly to Tyler, offering his hand. 'Tyler, we meet at last, though I feel I've known you for years. Your mother and I have followed your career with a great deal of pride over the years. I'm delighted for this opportunity to meet you in the flesh.'

Tyler was too much the gentleman to do anything so churlish as to ignore the out-stretched hand. 'Mr Wheeler. I've ... heard of you, naturally,' he returned smoothly. His attention turned to the elderly woman who stood silently by. 'Mother.' There was no warmth. He was greeting a stranger, and as he did so he eased free of Claudia's hold.

'Tyler,' she responded equally smoothly. 'You live in a beautiful part of the world.'

'It suits me.' His manners were impeccable but remote.

'Can I get you something to drink? Tea, or coffee?' Claudia offered.

Nancy shook her head. 'No, thank you, my dear; we stopped on the way.' Half turning, she observed her son with a mocking look that was so reminiscent of Tyler that Claudia gasped faintly. 'Dutch courage, I think you'd call it, Tyler,' she said challengingly.

He raised one eyebrow. 'Would I? Do you know me well enough to gauge my reactions?'

Nancy bore the recrimination with admirable fortitude. 'I know you better than you think, my son. I half expected you not to be here.'

Tyler's smile was cool. 'If I'd known of your intentions I would have saved you a wasted journey. However, your accomplice kept very quiet about it.' He threw Claudia a dark look.

Nancy witnessed it, and frowned deeply. 'Tyler, you're a grown man now, not a little boy too young to understand what's happening. Twenty years is a long time to bear a grudge. I came to put that right,' she rejoined sternly.

Claudia wondered how Tyler would take the maternal reproof. She bit her lip, hoping that Nancy knew what she was doing. Tyler could be so unpredictable.

His smile had never reminded her so much of a crocodile contemplating dinner. 'Do you think you can?'

Showing her mettle, his mother was undaunted. 'I *know* I can.' She removed her arm from that of Oscar, who sent Claudia a rather knowing grin, and she realised that there was more of Tyler in Nancy than she had suspected. Her nervousness had gone now that battle was at last enjoined.

Claudia cleared her throat. 'Why don't we all sit down?' she suggested, indicating the table and chairs on the patio. 'I'll get Mary to make tea anyway. It's such a hot day that I think we could all do with it.' She knew she could, even if it had been the depths of winter.

When she returned to take her seat after relaying the message she found Tyler had manoeuvred himself as far away from his mother as possible. Her heart sank. Why did he have to make it so difficult?

Yet Nancy didn't seem to notice. 'You're looking well, Tyler.'

Sitting with one ankle supported on the other knee, he looked relaxed. 'So do you, but then money does tend to soften the ravages of time, doesn't it?'

Clearly to his surprise, Nancy laughed. 'I expect it does, but I wouldn't know. Until I married Oscar I had worked all my life. First on the farm, and you know how hard that was. Then after I left the sanatorium I took every job I could get just to survive. When I married Donald I worked because I felt it important to have an identity of my own. Hollywood can be a graveyard for marriages. Ours worked well, so much so that I wasn't afraid to seek happiness again after he died.'

Tyler didn't look particularly impressed. 'As I recall, he left you a very wealthy woman.'

'For all of five minutes,' Oscar corrected, reaching out to clasp his wife's hand. 'There's a great deal to admire in your mother, Tyler. Her strength and her generosity. She donated Donald's fortune to cancer research. A noble gesture from a noble woman.'

'Rubbish! I had the house and my job. I didn't need the money, and it could be put to far better use, helping those who suffered like Donald,' Nancy replied dismissively.

'You and Claudia have a great deal in common,' Tyler observed.

'More than you'd suppose. We had husbands whose behaviour was totally unreasonable. Thankfully Claudia got out in time, or who knows what would have happened?' his mother enlarged.

Tyler's expression became granite-like. 'Naturally you'd applaud anyone who followed your example,' he said coldly, and Claudia's heart sank.

Blue eyes, so like her son's, held his steadily. 'Good heavens, no, I'm pleased to say. I left it much too late. Kit's jealousy drove me to a nervous breakdown. Claudia was spared that. Ah, tea!' Nancy exclaimed softly as Mary appeared with a trolley. 'Just what the doctor ordered.'

Tyler was very quiet as they drank their tea. Nancy had adroitly changed the subject, chatting to Claudia about how the concert tour had gone so far. Clearly she had her strategy worked out. She had vouchsafed certain information; if Tyler wanted to know more then he would have to ask. Whether the seeds of doubt had been sown on fertile ground or not remained to be seen.

After a while Nancy put her cup down and looked at her son. 'There are some things I would like you to look at, Tyler. Whether you do so or not is up to you, but I'll leave them with you all the same. Oscar, would you mind getting that package from the car?' She watched as he strode away down the lawn before continuing. 'I came today because I knew this could be my last chance to see you.

I would have come years ago if you'd answered my letters.'

'Your memory's a little faulty, isn't it? It was my letters you never answered,' Tyler returned quickly.

Nancy sighed. 'We both wrote, Tyler, but neither got the letters. Why do you suppose that was?'

Tyler frowned. 'Are you suggesting my grandparents intercepted them? I don't believe it! Why would they do such a thing?'

'Because they never liked me. Because they wanted to keep us apart, and keep you.'

Tyler opened his mouth, then shut it again without a word. He sat back, his gaze somewhere across the field as he frowned, deep in thought.

Claudia swiftly stepped into the breach. 'You mentioned being in a sanatorium just now,' she said, and Tyler looked round sharply.

Nancy nodded gratefully. 'Yes; yes, I did. The irony of it was that I collapsed on my way to get you, Tyler. When I left there six months later you were with your father. I didn't abandon you, though it must have seemed like it. But, of course, by then it was too late. You didn't answer my letters, and when Kit died his parents persuaded me you were better off with them. Because I loved you I had to agree. I don't expect you'll believe me—it's been so long—but I never meant to hurt you, Tyler. I loved you very much, and I always have.' Oscar returned with a large package which Nancy took with a smile. 'Thank you, darling.' She set it before her son. 'These are for you to read if you want to. If you ever decide to hear my side then my address is there, too. You don't have to decide today or even next year, but, Tyler, until I die it will never be too late—remember that.' There was a glitter in her eyes as she stood up. 'Now I think we should go before we outstay our welcome. Claudia, my dear, I hope we meet again very soon. I should have liked to meet Natalie; she sounds delightful.' Once more she turned to her son. 'Tyler, pride is cold comfort. Don't turn your back on happiness for anything I might have done. You'll live to regret it if you do. Goodbye, son; I wish you well.'

In no time at all Claudia had kissed both Nancy and Oscar goodbye and was waving them off down the road. Choked with emotion, she glanced up to where Tyler still stood like a statue by the table. He hadn't responded to his mother's words, and she knew that Nancy had felt she had failed, despite the brave face she wore.

Slowly she made her way back to him. He was staring woodenly after the car and didn't appear aware of her presence. Yet when she reached out and touched his arm he shrugged her off distastefully.

'Don't touch me, Claudia,' he warned, menacingly soft.

'Tyler, please —— '

'I don't want to hear anything you have to say either. You've said and done quite enough for one afternoon,' he added scathingly.

She squared her shoulders, knowing he was bound to take out whatever he was feeling on her. 'Will you at least look at the things your mother left?'

His blue gaze was savage. 'If you want to know what's in them you'll have to open them yourself,' he bit out through clenched teeth, then turned his back on her pointedly and strode angrily away.

Claudia chewed her lip. He was justifiably angry because he hated to be manoeuvred into anything. But she still felt it had had to be done. Glancing down at the table, she eyed the plainly wrapped package. If Nancy had brought it along she obviously felt it was important, perhaps even vital. Which gave her every reason for opening it herself. After all, Tyler had given her *his* permission, albeit angrily.

The brown paper, once removed, revealed two large black padded albums. After turning over one or two pages, Claudia sank on to a chair, absorbed by the contents. If anything could reveal just how much Nancy loved her son then this did. For the albums were scrapbooks, beginning with Tyler's birth certificate and containing even the smallest mention of him as a member of the school rugger team, through every article ever written about him, up to the present day. And by the side of each were Nancy's written comments, so poignant, so proud, that it made Claudia want to weep for them both.

She knew then that it was absolutely vital that Tyler should see them himself, and she knew exactly where to find him. Cradling them in her arms, she made her way purposefully to the study. She went in without bothering to knock, striding to the desk where he sat, and dumped them down before him. He had been staring out of the window, but he turned at her entry. Opening the top album randomly, her finger jabbed at the page.

'If you never do anything else for your mother, Tyler, read that. Read it, and if you can't do so without realising that you were wrong, very, very wrong, then I'll know you can never be the man I love,' she declared passionately.

Without another word she spun on her heel and left. She had done all she could do; the rest was up to him.

CHAPTER NINE

CLAUDIA!

The echoing memory of her name drew Claudia up from a deep sleep with a sickening lurch of shock. She sat up quickly, head swimming from the sudden movement, blinking owlishly in the darkness, trying to recall just what had disturbed her. All was quiet now, but her thumping heart told her something must have happened. She groped for her travel alarm on the bedside table and saw, by the light of the open window, that it was close on three o'clock in the morning.

Thinking that perhaps Natalie had called out to her, Claudia slid her legs over the edge of the bed and reached for her silk wrap. It was a sultry night, and she had dispensed with her nightdress in favour of the coolness of only a sheet for covering. For a moment the moonlight glinted on dewed skin, then the rounded hips and full breasts were hidden from view as she tied the belt about her narrow waist.

She padded barefoot down the hallway to Natalie's room and peeped in. Her daughter was fast asleep, arms thrown wide for coolness, and the absence of Wendy proved that it hadn't been she who had called out. She closed the door again, deciding that whatever had roused her had probably been part of her own dreams. But, just as she was stepping inside her own room, a deep moan echoed down from the other end of the hall. Goosebumps chased up and down her spine as the eerie sound wrenched at her nerves, setting them vibrantly on end. Unearthly as it sounded, she knew where it came from.

On silent feet she travelled the length of the passage to halt outside Tyler's door, listening intently. She hadn't seen him since those moments in the study after lunch. He hadn't emerged for dinner, and Mary had reported that he hadn't eaten what she had taken him. Neither had he appeared before she had gone to bed herself, close on midnight. Yet clearly he had come upstairs some time after that.

Not to sleep peacefully, though. Through the thickness of the wood she could hear vague mutterings, and then a harshly uttered 'No!' jarred on her senses and propelled her into the room, closing the door softly behind her.

Tyler was lying on the bed, body moving restlessly against the silken sheet, muttering under his breath. At one point he had been covered by a sheet, but his wild threshing had sent it to the floor and his body lay naked before her, pooled in the silver glow of the moon. He was bathed in sweat, so every powerful muscle was outlined in the silky light. His broad chest, with its matting of darkened hair, tapered down to a flat stomach and powerful loins, narrow hips and long athletic legs. It was a starkly erotic sight that set Claudia's pulse tripping madly and started a throb of longing in the very depth of her body.

'No, Claudia! Don't go!' Tyler's cry of despair jolted her back to awareness of what she was doing there.

Overwhelmed by the knowledge that she was part of what he was reliving, Claudia raised her hand and smoothed away the tangled locks of damp hair from his forehead and cheeks. 'Wake up, Tyler, wake up!'

Restless hands reached for hers immediately, grasping them with a strength he was unaware of, drawing her down across his chest. 'Don't leave me, Claudia! Come back!'

Trapped, Claudia steeled her rioting senses at this unforeseen closeness, and tried again. 'I'm here, darling. I'm not going anywhere. Do you hear me, Tyler? You're just having a bad dream!'

Slowly his hands relaxed their hold on her wrists. Staring down into his face, she saw him blink.

'Claudia?' His voice was husky and confused.

She licked dry lips to moisten them. 'Yes, it's me. You called out in your sleep. You were having a nightmare.'

'A nightmare? Oh, God, yes...I remember,' he muttered thickly.

'Yes...well...' Claudia reluctantly began to ease away from him, but, even as she took that first tentative inch, Tyler's arms glided round her, holding her fast. She froze, eyes locked with his. 'It's over; you can let me go now,' she ordered breathily.

His blue eyes were hooded and smouldering. 'You said you weren't going anywhere,' he reminded her. 'I don't want you to go.'

Pressed so intimately close to him, she could feel his body underlining his words and moaned as her own body wanted to melt. 'I *must* go.'

'No, you belong here, with me,' he insisted throatily.

She closed her eyes against the temptation of his. 'Tyler, this isn't fair.'

'Claudia, tonight I need you more than I've needed anyone in my whole life.'

Opening her eyes, she looked deeply into his and was lost. 'Tyler...'

'Don't go...please. Stay with me.' His voice became a husky throb. 'Let me love you,' he pleaded, and her resistance crumpled.

The room instantly became hot and airless as his hardening body spoke of his need of her, and her own desire was not proof against it. Senses clamouring wildly, she slid her legs down the bed and allowed her body to come into full contact with his. His hand drew her head down to his, and it was like being in the grip of some powerful narcotic. His mouth was hot, his invading tongue joining with hers in an erotic mime, savouring the depth, taste and feel of her.

It was so good! The electric response of her senses shot all caution to the four winds as they started out on a path of discovery. With eager lips Claudia sought out the hills and valleys of his face, while his hand slid down beneath the short silk robe and closed over her rounded buttocks, pulling her down to meet the pulsing urgency of his desire.

Gently Tyler pushed her on to her back, divesting her of the flimsy covering of her robe. As he dropped the offending garment to the floor, Claudia slid her arms around him and arched her back, urging her achingly swollen breasts against the silky mat of hair on his chest. The effect was shockingly sensual, drawing a growl of pleasure from Tyler's throat and an answering gasp of delight from her.

His lips foraged, tracing a line down her throat until she was shivering in his arms, and then her senses concentrated sharply as his free hand began a journey of its own. The feel of his warm skin moving over her sent a tremor of excitement through her, melting her bones and setting every nerve quivering.

Tyler had magic in his touch, playing her like a finely tuned instrument. Down her silky thigh his hand travelled, conquering her by inches. Lazily it climbed back upwards along her inner thigh, and he moved one lean leg between hers. As he sought and found his goal, circling and stroking, sending shock waves of intense pleasure along her veins, Tyler's lips retraced their path to hers. Hotly his mouth moulded itself to hers and took up the rhythm of his fingers.

A low moan forced its way from her throat and her hands clutched his shoulders as she returned his kiss, her tense body arching to meet his hand as a storm of sensation broke in waves upon her. She tore her mouth away, gasping. Through a mist she saw Tyler smile

slowly before his head descended to the frant-
ically beating pulse at the base of her throat.

His subtle hands and lips discovered the
hidden places that could arouse her to fever-
pitch. Like now. His hands skated upwards,
grazing her breasts, feeling her quiver of
desire, but ignoring the unspoken plea of her
arched back. His fingers traced a line around
the base of each surging peak until Claudia
could stand the teasing not one second longer,
and her hand dropped to cover his and urge
it on to her inflamed skin.

With a deep moan she welcomed his touch
as his fingers began to rub and knead, his
thumb tantalising her nipple into a proud
nubbin. From far away she heard Tyler
chuckle.

'You devil!' Claudia gasped on a sigh that
changed to a moan of pleasure as his head
lowered, drawing the proud peak into the
moist cavern of his mouth, suckling there
until she was in a delirium before transferring
his attention to the twin mound.

She felt incredibly bereft when his head
lifted away, her body quivering at the ces-
sation of such heady pleasure. Her hands rose
to pull him back to her, but Tyler removed
himself completely, lying on his back beside
her. Claudia raised herself on to her elbow,

her lovely eyes searching his for an answer to his retreat. A shock ran through her as she met the blaze of desire in his eyes.

'Touch me, Claudia. How I ache for the feel of your hands!'

Claudia looked down the length of his glistening body. Lingeringly she let her wanton hands wander where they would, conscious of every quiver of pleasure beneath her fingers, and the stifled sounds that issued from between his tightly drawn lips.

Her boldness amazed her. Only with Tyler did she feel able to express her love so sensuously. Gordon had frozen her; Tyler set her free. Free to experience the power of her nature. Lovingly she sought to return in full measure the gratification he had given her, but when his husky groans and trembling warned her he could not accept much more she retreated in her turn until she could look down into his smouldering eyes.

'You have the power to drive a man mad.'

'My pleasure.'

'Oh, no, darling, ours—definitely ours,' he declared, pulling her down.

With a sigh Claudia subsided over him, her lips seeking his as her body moved of its own accord against the hardness of his. When he rolled over to pin her beneath him, gliding between her thighs, they were both shaking with the need to end the tension they had created.

Claudia could no longer think clearly. In an agony of wanting she arched her body to his and accepted the thrust that made them one. She could feel the tension in his quivering muscles as he tried to hold back, but their need was too great. With a groan he lost control, plunging them both into the white-hot inferno, rushing even higher on a spiralling wave of almost intolerable pleasure until finally, with mingled cries, they hurtled into space. Senses ravished, they floated free, the echo of their hearts beating as one the only reminder of their mortality.

For long minutes they lay in silence, their spent bodies unable to move. At last Tyler found the strength to shift his weight from her, and Claudia shivered as the cooler air passed over the heated flesh of their sweat-soaked bodies. Her lids felt weighted in the aftermath of a union so completely satisfying, yet she did not want to sleep, lest she lose the wonder of the moment. Tyler settled his head into her shoulder, and she could feel his breath stirring the hair against her neck.

Dreamily her hand stroked him. Her heart was full. There was so much she wanted to say to him.

'Tyler.' She murmured his name, but he didn't stir, and, tipping her head, she saw that his eyes were closed, his face relaxed in sleep. A smile curved her lips. Never mind, there was always tomorrow. With a soft sigh she let sleep take her too.

Dust motes floated in the shaft of sunlight that drew Claudia from the realms of sleep into a brand-new day. Outside the window she could hear the clear call of a peewit haunting the air.

A delicious lethargy remained as testimony of the happenings of the night. She stretched sinuously, moving with unconscious grace against the cool sheets, and turned her head on the pillow, only to discover that Tyler had already left the bed.

Disappointment wiped the smile from her eyes. Why had he left without stirring her? She would have liked to greet him in privacy, perhaps even have made love with him once more. Last night had been special, a new beginning. Of course, that hadn't changed, but she would have been happier with the reassuring presence of his warm body beside her.

Keeping the sheet about her, she sat up and glanced at the alarm. Ten o'clock. No wonder Tyler had left her. He would have been at work hours ago! He probably thought he was doing her a favour, not realising that she would rather have the reassurance of his presence, even if only at breakfast. Now she would have to wait until lunch or brave his wrath and interrupt him in his study. A sensuous smiled curved her lips. She didn't think he would mind the interruption, not today.

Holding the thought, she slipped from the bed and shrugged into her robe, returning to her own room. Ten minutes later, invigorated by a cool shower and dressed in turquoise shorts and a white sleeveless T-shirt, she made her way downstairs.

Claudia couldn't hear Natalie or Wendy, but the sound of someone singing drew her to the kitchen. Mary was busy kneading dough. She glanced up with a smile, dusting off her hands.

'Good morning, Mary. Isn't it an absolutely wonderful day?' she greeted chirpily.

Mary's smile became a beam. 'My, my, you're very happy this morning! Coffee?' She turned to the percolator.

Claudia grinned. 'Two cups, please. I'll have mine with Tyler. And yes, I am happy. Very, very happy,' she agreed.

'Well,' the housekeeper exclaimed, filling two cups, 'I must say it's about time! You take these and run along. I'll see you're not disturbed.'

Dropping a kiss on Mary's cheek, Claudia took the cups. 'You're a treasure!'

Happiness bubbling away inside her, she made her way to the study. Elbowing open the door, she smiled at Tyler as he looked up, frowning.

'Hi—coffee break,' she declared, shoving the door to and advancing to deposit both cups on the desk. Then she circled behind him, slipping her arms round his neck. 'Good morning, darling.' Her lips caressed his cheek. 'I missed you. Why didn't you wake me?'

Tyler tipped his head away. 'I imagined you wanted to sleep.'

She laughed huskily, fingers slipping inside his shirt. 'I wanted you more than sleep.'

His hands came up to fasten about her wrists. 'Stop it, Claudia. I don't have time for this,' he said repressively.

'There's always time for this,' she teased, and would have said more only she found herself being thrust away.

'I said no, Claudia!' he repeated, getting up and moving away from her.

Stunned, she stared at him, arms falling to her sides. 'I don't understand. Last night...'

Tyler grimaced. 'Was last night. This morning I'm too busy to fool around.'

Ice seemed to settle about her heart. 'Fool around?' she exclaimed, eyes fixed on his closed face. 'We made love, we didn't fool around!'

He drew in a breath. 'Maybe that was a mistake, but —— '

Pain lanced through her. 'You used me!' she cried, cutting him off.

A nerve ticked in his jaw. 'Claudia, I don't have time for this now!' he grated, glancing at his watch.

She felt sick. 'No, you had all you wanted last night! I fell for it hook, line and sinker! You aren't the man I thought you were at all!' With a muffled cry she turned and ran to the door, ignoring his cry for her to stop. She had to get away before she made a complete and utter fool of herself.

On the patio she stopped abruptly, brought up short by the sight of the housekeeper, who paused in her cleaning to look up in surprise. But before either could say a word a footfall behind Claudia had her freezing. She didn't need to turn to know it was Tyler, yet she faced him anyway, eyes flashing bitterly. Expression shuttered, he carried a coat and a holdall.

'I have to leave now, and I don't know when I'll be back. I don't have time to explain,' he said shortly.

Claudia shrugged. 'There's no need; I understand.'

About to say something, he clamped his lips and changed his mind. 'I'll be in touch.'

She smiled acidly. 'Natalie will be pleased.'

Swearing under his breath, he shot her a fulminating look. 'To hell with it!' he snapped, and turned and walked away. A few minutes later she saw him drive away.

'And to hell with you, too, Tyler Monroe!' she whispered after him, fighting back tears. Hating him, hating herself, because she knew she had been the most utter fool. To believe that Tyler really cared, that last night had meant something. Oh, it meant something all right! That he had wanted her—and had her! That stung the most. That she had been stupid enough to believe he really needed her.

'Whatever's happened?' Mary asked, coming over to her.

Claudia gritted her teeth. 'He didn't want the coffee.'

Mary clucked her tongue. 'I take it you argued. Whatever it was about, I'm sure Mr Tyler can put it right when he comes back.'

Claudia shivered, hugging her arms about her. 'I doubt it.'

'Of course he will. He loves you, doesn't he?' Mary chivvied her.

'Does he?' She knew better—now.

'Oh, I know he doesn't like to admit it, but I'm sure he does. You'll just have to get him to show it,' the housekeeper advised.

Claudia's laugh was bitter. 'I thought I had.'

'Men aren't easy to understand, but you're a woman. There are ways of getting him to show his hand,' Mary encouraged, and Claudia sighed.

'I know you mean well, Mary, but you don't understand.' She gave her a tight smile. 'I think I'll go for a walk.'

The housekeeper watched her walk away thoughtfully. After a while her expression lightened. Sometimes people needed a little push. Humming, she went back to her work.

The next few days were dismal as Claudia brooded over what she saw as her rank stupidity. She felt she had betrayed herself by giving in so easily, and if he had used her then it had been with her consent. Which only made her feel worse.

At the same time she was very much aware that Natalie and Wendy realised something momentous had happened, though they couldn't imagine what. The result was that Natalie took to sticking to her like glue. She appreciated their concern and responded to it by making a determined effort to be cheerful. Something that proved easier as the days went by.

Around that time she became aware of Natalie and Wendy having several whispered conversations. She guessed they were plotting something, but her natural inquisitiveness was blunted by deeper issues. She had made a decision. When Tyler returned she would leave. She had already contacted several estate agents and asked for details of properties.

She couldn't say it made her feel happier, but her pride made it necessary. To remain might give him the idea she was willing to indulge in an affair. Which was definitely not the case. So it felt like the end of something, not the beginning of a new life with her daughter. Still, she put on as brave a face as she could for Natalie's sake.

A week after Tyler had gone she took her breakfast outside and settled herself in a sunny spot on the patio. She had barely sat down when she heard Natalie's voice calling her as she and Wendy made their way up the lawn. Quickly she summoned a smile, that empty region inside her feeling smaller as she received her daughter's swift embrace.

'I thought you'd never get up!' Natalie complained, sitting down and swiping half a slice of toast off her mother's plate.

'It's not that late,' Claudia protested, although she had slept in. She smiled at Wendy as she came up to join them.

'I know, but there was something I especially wanted to ask you,' Natalie said with her mouth full. 'I've been waiting hours!'

Claudia bit back a laugh. 'Oh, dear, I'm so sorry. If I'd known I wouldn't have slept at all!'

Natalie grinned, then sobered swiftly. 'Seriously, Mamma, do say yes; I told Wendy you wouldn't mind.'

With a mother's instinct Claudia automatically became suspicious. 'Oh, you did, did you? I'm not saying yes until I know what I'm saying yes to.'

'The seaside!' Natalie declared despairingly, as if it had been painfully obvious all the time. 'Why don't we go to Wales? Tyler has a cottage we could use. It's so hot here. Could we go, please?' she begged, eyes huge and hopeful.

'The seaside?' Claudia murmured doubtfully, glancing at Wendy, who shrugged.

'I don't see why not. Natalie's well. It will
probably do her good if we don't overdo it.
But I told her it was up to you.'

Claudia nodded but didn't answer at once.
A cottage by the sea. The idea was appealing.
It could be just what she needed to take her
mind off things. Tyler could hardly complain
when he had disappeared without a word,
leaving her in charge. Besides, if she was going
to be independent, she might as well start
now. She gave Natalie a broad smile.

'Why not? I think it's a wonderful idea.
Just the three of us. We could have a bar-
becue, or anything else you fancy.'

Natalie jumped to her feet to throw her
arms around her mother's neck, half throt-
tling her. 'Oh, great! I knew you'd say yes.
When can we go—today?'

Claudia was swept along by her enthusiasm. 'I don't see why we shouldn't, if the
cottage is habitable. Of course, we'll have to
get packed in time, and then there's the food.'

'I'll go and tell Mary. She'll pack us a
hamper full of stuff!' Natalie declared.
Behind her mother's back she gave Wendy a
broad grin and a thumbs-up sign before

rushing off. She could be heard calling the housekeeper as she ran through the house.

Sighing, Claudia locked glances with Wendy and both burst out laughing.

'Perhaps it wasn't such a good idea,' Claudia said wryly.

Wendy rose with a grin. 'Oh, I don't know; I think it will do us all good. I'd better start packing or Natalie will be unbearable.'

Claudia drained the last of her coffee and rose too. 'In that case, I'd better join you,' she declared, and they walked inside, making their hurried plans.

The cottage was very old. Built from mellow stone and roofed with the finest Welsh slate, it nestled against the hillside at the end of a quiet lane. Love and care had been lavished on creating a garden in which wild flowers were encouraged to grow. Rambling roses climbed the walls, and framed the lower windows. Beyond the garden a pathway led round the curve of the hill to where, faintly, could be heard the rhythmic sound of the ocean.

Natalie was out of the car as soon as Claudia brought it to a halt, disappearing to search out old haunts. The two women climbed out more slowly. Claudia dug out from her bag the key Mary had produced and led the way up the path to the front door. It opened directly into a large, airy living-room. A doorway led to a kitchen, which doubled as dining area. Another door revealed a steep staircase, leading up to three bedrooms, two fairly large, and the other little more than a shoebox, plus the bathroom.

Natalie returned while they were exploring, and together all three set about unpacking the cases and the food, and generally getting settled in. Then they all traipsed off to the beach for an hour or two before tea, by which time Natalie was already yawning, tired out by the travelling and sheer excitement. She put up no protest when urged up to bed.

By ten o'clock Claudia found herself unable to stifle her jaw-breaking yawns any longer. Wendy had given up long since, and now Claudia locked up and climbed the stairs to her room. Within ten minutes she was in bed, falling asleep virtually as soon as her head touched the pillow.

The next few days followed the same pattern. They haunted the beach, only returning to the cottage to eat, and by eleven at night all were sleeping soundly. Claudia didn't allow herself any time to think or brood. There were still household chores to be done,

and she took on most of them herself, waving
away Wendy's offers of help. For there was a
method in her madness. Worn out, she slept
dreamlessly until the sunlight woke her in the
morning.

By the middle of the week, when she took
Natalie into town to replenish the cupboards,
Claudia was congratulating herself that she
had done the right thing. She had hardly
thought of Tyler at all—well, only once or
twice a day. It would get better, for she had
set her mind to it. He needn't think that because she had succumbed once he was on to
a good thing. She refused to be caught in that
particular trap. For her own self-respect it had
to be all or nothing. Once in her life she had
been used as a convenience, but never again.
Her heart might weep, but she was more than
just a body.

The shopping completed, Claudia allowed
Natalie to show her over the ruins of a once-
magnificent castle, after which they bought
some cans of Coke, spicy chicken and fries
and picnicked happily on the beach. They
struggled, laughing uproariously, to con-
struct a sandcastle without the aid of bucket
and spade. The last remnants of Natalie's reserve had melted away like ice in the sun, and

now, day by day, they were forging links that nothing could destroy.

They sang songs on the journey home, arriving just as a small army of men went out to mow a meadow. Wendy was just setting the phone down as the two of them carried the groceries inside.

'Was that for me?' Claudia asked as she put down the heavy box-load. The thought that it might have been Tyler made her heart jump, until she saw Wendy shake her head.

'No, Mrs Peterson,' the nanny explained, smiling at Natalie as she came to help unpack. 'Actually I was speaking to my mother.' She paused uncertainly. 'I don't know if I told you that she lives not very far away? My parents have a farm.' She lifted out a jar and studied it as if it had the power to speak. 'Er—I know it's a bit of a liberty, but I was wondering if you wouldn't mind if I visited them tonight. It would mean borrowing the car. I could stay overnight and come back in the morning.'

'Of course I don't mind, Wendy. In fact, I should have thought of it before. You never seem to take half the time that's due you. Take the car and welcome,' Claudia insisted at once.

'Thanks. There is just one other thing. Would it be possible to take Natalie with me?

I promised I'd take her to see the animals one day. It is only five miles away down the valley, so she wouldn't be far.'

Claudia blinked, a little taken aback, but she happened to catch the expectant look on her daughter's face as she hopped from one foot to the other, and knew she just couldn't say no. After all, it would only be for a few hours.

She laughed ruefully. 'Somehow I don't think my life would be worth living if I said no. All right, you may go, but you're to be on your best behaviour, Natalie, or you won't be asked back again,' she cautioned.

'I'll be good, I promise,' Natalie responded with a grin.

'Hmm,' Claudia murmured doubtfully and held out her hand. 'Come along, let's pack your things. And you'd better change into jeans and your trainers. If I remember correctly, farms can be awfully mucky places. I'm sure you're going to have great fun!'

An hour later she waved them both off. Her smile faded as the silence fell around her. She felt abandoned, which was silly because Natalie would be back tomorrow—she hadn't gone forever. It was a hangover from the past, one she doubted she would ever really get over.

For now, though, she shrugged it off determinedly, spending the remainder of the afternoon mowing the lawn and returning some sort of order to the flowerbeds. Having surveyed her handiwork with satisfaction, she went indoors, drew herself a bath, poured in a generous helping of her favourite bath oil, and treated herself to a long, leisurely soak.

Later, clad in her silk robe, she washed and dried her hair, made herself some coffee and sandwiches, and took them into the lounge, settling down on the couch with a book. But Claudia had barely opened it at the first chapter when the peace of the valley was broken by the sound of a car accelerating down the lane towards the cottage. Frowning, she lowered her book, wondering who it could be.

The most logical assumption, considering the time, was a stray motorist on the wrong road, which they would soon discover it to be, for the lane ended abruptly at her door. It had already happened once or twice during their short stay, and they had been called upon to point the wanderer in the right direction for the town. Not a hazard during the day, but at night it was a different matter.

Claudia glanced down at her robe, which was all she wore, realising it was hardly the best item of clothing in which to receive strangers. However, there was no time to run up and change, for, even as she considered it, the car had scrunched to a halt and the driver's footsteps could be heard advancing up the path. The sharp knock on the door startled her, even though she had been expecting it.

She climbed to her feet, automatically tightening the belt. As her hand reached for the bolt an idea struck her, and she raised her voice. 'Natalie, keep the dog in the kitchen, please.' Hoping that that was warning enough that she wasn't alone in the house, she released the bolt.

Pulling the door open, her words of enquiry died unuttered on her lips as the identity of her caller was revealed.

'Tyler!'

CHAPTER TEN

'YES, Tyler,' he agreed in a voice like thunder, and, stepping forward, urged Claudia backwards by the sheer force of his presence. The door closed firmly behind him.

Stunned, she could only stare at him. His face was etched with lines of tiredness, but his predominant emotion was anger. His hair showed evidence of violent mistreatment, and his rigid body indicated strong feelings held sternly in check. Recalling how they had parted, she was at a loss to understand, then realisation dawned. She had flouted his command and he didn't like it.

Anger came to her defence. She had rights too. He needn't think he could browbeat her just because she hadn't asked his permission to take Natalie away!

'Running away again, Claudia? It appears to be becoming a habit with you!' he ground out tersely.

The accusation so surprised her that she had no chance of avoiding the two strong hands that reached out to manacle her shoulders, biting deeply into her tender flesh.

But the savage shaking her bemused mind expected did not follow. Instead she was jerked forwards until she fell against the hard, uncompromising wall of his chest.

One hand released her shoulder to imprison a handful of sweet-scented hair, tugging her head back until it could go no further, and she was left gazing helplessly up at him, absolutely, totally confused by the turn of events.

'God, I could kill you,' Tyler muttered thickly. 'This is the last time you ever run away from me. Understand me, Claudia? The last time.'

She *didn't* understand; she only knew she had to pacify him. 'Yes. Yes, I understand,' she said huskily, and immediately found herself drawn more closely against his taut body, her reeling head pressed into his shoulder. Dear heaven, he was holding her as if he would never let her go!

Above her, Tyler groaned. 'Why the hell did you do it? Because I went away? But I told you I'd be back. Where else could I go? Hell, Claudia, I know I've never said it, but I thought you knew.'

To Claudia it was like wandering through a maze, blindfold. All she knew was what she could feel—the riot of emotions trembling within him. 'Knew what?' she whispered, seeking the light.

'That I loved you. That I'd finally stopped denying how much I needed you,' he revealed in a voice that couldn't hide the truth of his words. 'When I returned home, and Mary told me you'd gone, I couldn't believe it. Yet when I found you'd taken everything with you I was devastated. I thought I'd lost you for good, and it was all my own fault for being so blind and stubborn.'

Claudia took in a wavery breath. Mary had told him she had gone? Had hidden her belongings to uphold the lie? It was incredible. Yet not as incredible as the fact that, believing it, Tyler had come in hot pursuit! Her heart leapt. 'I see. And then Mary told you I was here?' she said unevenly, forced to keep up the housekeeper's charade because understanding was bursting around her like a fireworks display. He loved her. He really did love her!

Tyler released her sufficiently to be able to look down into her face. 'Don't be angry with her. When she saw how cut up I was she told me she thought I might stand one last chance. That if I told you exactly how I felt you might change your mind. I know I haven't given you much reason to trust me, but if you come back

I promise you'll never have to doubt again that I love you.'

Twice now he had said the words she had never thought to hear. She knew she should tell him what Mary had done, but somehow it just didn't seem important. She forgot the hurt, forgot everything but what her eyes and heart were telling her. 'Do you still want to kill me?' she asked softly, her eyes warm and luminous as she looked at him.

He shook his head, swallowing to ease a constriction in his throat. 'No, I want to marry you, just as soon as it can be arranged. Will you?'

Confident at last, Claudia eased one arm free and raised her hand to cup his cheek gently. 'I love you. Don't you know I want to spend my life with you, grow old with you? Yes, I'll marry you.'

Tyler lowered lids over eyes that glittered, his hand covering hers as he pressed his lips against her palm. 'Thank you. You won't regret it.'

'I've never regretted loving you, Tyler, and I never could.'

He raised his head and smiled at her. 'I agree with Mary, I don't deserve you.'

'Mary's a wonderful woman, but she isn't always right,' she disagreed. But she had known how to manipulate Tyler! 'You look tired.'

Tyler grimaced. 'I feel exhausted, but it was worth it,' he declared.

Claudia eased herself free of his arms, feeling rather guilt-stricken. 'I'd just made myself coffee and sandwiches. Why don't you take your jacket off and make yourself comfortable while I get you some?' she suggested. 'Will cheese and tomato be all right?' she asked as she watched him shrug off his jacket and fold his long length into a corner of the couch, flexing the muscles of his neck and shoulders wearily.

He looked up with a smile. 'That would be great, thanks.'

'Won't be a minute, then.' Claudia took a step towards the kitchen then swung round again. 'Oh, about Natalie —— ' she began, but Tyler cut her off.

'It's OK, she knows nothing about this. Mary had Wendy take her to see her parents' farm.'

Claudia's jaw showed a tendency to drop. 'Oh, that's all right, then,' she said lamely and left him. In the kitchen she shook her head wonderingly. The only way Mary could know about the farm outing was if it had all been carefully arranged. Now she had no doubt that, if Wendy was in on the plot, then Natalie was, too. She supposed she should be angry. They had gambled that Tyler would come after her, but what if he hadn't? Yet they had been right, so they must have seen what she hadn't—that he loved her. So how could she be angry?

Later, after they had eaten their simple meal and were sitting together on the couch, Claudia attempted to explain.

'Tyler, about my leaving...' she began tentatively.

Turning to her, he took her hands in his. 'There's nothing to explain. It was a lesson I needed to learn. To really know the value of something you have to come close to losing it, you said, and it's true. I don't want to face life without you. And Natalie.' His expression became serious. 'I have a request to make. It would please me very much if, once we were married, I could adopt Natalie. Would you object?'

Claudia abandoned her explanations, flooded by emotions that clogged her voice. 'Of course I wouldn't, and we know it's what Natalie would like.'

Tyler's blue eyes were gentle. 'I want us to be a proper family, Claudia.'

She freed her hands, only to throw them about his neck, unshed tears making her eyes glisten. 'I want that too, very, very much. But I don't want her to be an only child. I want her to have brothers and sisters.'

His hands cupped her face, thumbs wiping away her tears. 'The way I feel about you,' he said huskily, 'I think that's a distinct possibility. I love you, Claudia. Never doubt it.'

For a long moment he stared at her, then he lowered his mouth to hers, pressing tender kisses to her lips until slowly Claudia returned them, acknowledging the mutual need to touch and taste. Her arms enfolded him, hands running up his back as their lips rubbed and teased, and sought again the blessing of each other.

Both were breathing heavily as they drew apart. Blue eyes glittered as he gazed down upon her upturned face. He took in the faint glow of colour beneath her fine skin, the yearning fullness of her lips, parted to show the merest glimpse of pearly teeth. The eyes that locked with his were sending out a message that needed no interpretation.

Tyler's response was immediate. With delicate movements he moved his hands, letting them glide down the arched perfection of her neck, lingering over the pulse that had started up a frantic throbbing at his practised touch. Silken skin shivered beneath his fingers as they moved down the deep V at the neck of her robe, easing the edges apart to bare the fullness of her breasts to the thrill of his touch and the warmth of his gaze.

When his hands cupped and weighed their swollen bounty, Claudia's breath caught in her throat and she closed her eyes as a fierce wave of longing swept over her. Nothing could ever equal the pleasure the feel of Tyler's hands upon her evoked. She could think only of the fever in her blood which pulsated to every pore, turning her bones to water and her nerve-ends into conductors of the powerful surge of desire which threatened to overcome her.

Tyler's tactile exploration continued to tease and caress her, sensitising her aching nipples into tight buds which registered every new touch with a rippling tide of voluptuous delight. With a tortured moan Claudia buried her head in Tyler's neck, pressing her lips to his skin in hot butterfly kisses up towards his ear. Gently she nipped the lobe, smiling as she registered his shuddering response, letting her tongue probe the maze-like coils until he too uttered a groan deep in his throat and returned her teasing in full measure.

Their breathing was far from steady as they drew apart to gaze deeply into one another's eyes, seeking and finding the answers to countless questions.

'I want you.' Tyler's voice was a husky rumble of sound. His hands, where they rested upon her, were unsteady, and the self-control he was imposing on himself trembled along the length of his body.

Claudia's mouth was so dry that she had to swallow in order to utter a few simple words. 'Love me.' With hands that shook as much as his she tried to undo his shirt, but her fingers were all thumbs, and it was Tyler who swiftly removed it; then he slipped to his knees before her. Deftly he untied the knot of her belt and slid the robe from her shoulders until it lay about her hips.

Large male hands closed about Claudia's waist and drew her down before him, creating a bubbling cauldron of warmth deep within her to match the heat of desire in Tyler's eyes. The intensity made her tremble, the sweet pulse of longing set up an insistent throbbing inside her, and it was with a gasp of pleasure that she gave herself into the strong arms encircling her. She moulded herself to Tyler's firm body, her arms stealing about his neck, her head thrown backwards as she delighted in the feel of his hands urging her hips towards the thrust of his.

Beneath her touch Claudia could feel Tyler's body vibrating in response to hers, drawing her closer between his knees, his dark head lowered until his seeking lips discovered one perfect jutting breast, and sucked the hardened nipple into the haven of his mouth. The havoc this sensual caress created subdued all other feelings. Her heart thundered like a trip-hammer, and tiny whimpers of pleasure forced their way from her throat.

It had never felt quite like this before— never! She wanted it to go on forever, this wild abandonment of self. Tyler was feeling it too, she knew it with every sensitised pore, and deep shudders were racking his frame. Glorying in the nuzzling, seeking lips, Claudia lowered her dark head down to his, her hands stealing slowly down the muscled planes of his back, following the line of his spine and up again to dig her hands into his hair and pull his mouth up to lock with hers.

Without recalling when they moved, Claudia became aware that they were lying down, and Tyler's hard, exciting body was pressing her back into the deep pile of the carpet. Instinctively she moved against him in a rhythm as old as time, inviting, begging, his possession. Breaking their kiss, Tyler raised himself enough to look down into her love-drugged face. His eyes traced every feature before settling on the fiery brown orbs.

'This isn't the most romantic place to make love,' he murmured huskily.

Quickly she shook her head. 'It is; oh, it is. Anywhere with you is perfect.'

'You don't want me to carry you upstairs?' His hands roved her shapely curves as he spoke, lingering on the velvety skin of her inner thigh.

'Uh-uh,' Claudia refused, 'I want you here and now. Make me yours again. I need you so much.' Her voice throbbed with the depth of her passion.

Tyler needed no more encouragement, and with a groan he moved away to remove the last of his clothing. Then he was with her again, gliding between her thighs, which parted to accommodate him, burning her up with the heat of his passion until the fire was out of control. Together their glistening bodies writhed and joined, seeking to savour every spark.

With a gasping cry of pleasure Claudia welcomed his thrusting possession, her knees grazing his waist as she strove to weld herself to him. She felt his hardness moving within her, exulting in each deep thrust carrying them upwards on a moaning wave of desire. Dizzying spirals threatened to send them careering into a vortex of excitement where every sense was strained to capture the moment of extreme satisfaction.

Her ecstatic cry was lost against Tyler's shoulder as his driving force triggered her to a climax of passion. Indescribable pleasure engulfed her, spinning her into space, conscious only of her pulsating body still moving with Tyler as he drove himself on to his own release, joining her finally in a wondrous free-fall through golden mists to the reality of the aftermath of passion.

As they basked in a hazy glow their laboured breathing gradually settled, and Claudia let her eyes remain closed as a voluptuous languor enfolded her. Their coming together had been perfect. Almost it seemed the first time for them, as if they had set out on a voyage of discovery and found a new world at the close.

Her sigh was very nearly a purr of delight.

Easing his weight to one side, but still with his head resting lightly on her breast, Tyler smiled. 'Happy?'

Claudia wound his hair around her finger. 'Wonderfully happy.'

For a while they said nothing more, content to lie in each other's arms and savour the closeness they had both thought was lost to them forever. But when the heat of passion had died away, leaving only faint embers burning, Claudia knew it was time to seek some answers.

'Why did you leave like that?' The minute the words left her she was aware of a new tension in Tyler. It was a minute or so before he spoke.

'Hell, I'm sorry I hurt you, Claudia. That night was perfect, but it made me question everything I thought I believed in. When you came to the study there was nothing more I wanted than to be with you, but there were things I had to do. Things I couldn't explain to you. What I couldn't tell you, Claudia, was that I was going to see my mother,' he told her gruffly.

Claudia's heart very nearly stopped. 'Oh, Tyler!'

Unconsciously his fingers tightened on her waist. 'When I saw her...when I read those albums...dear God, Claudia, I couldn't hold on to my hate any longer.' His voice was pained and she closed her eyes tightly.

'I knew you couldn't. You do believe she loves you?'

'If those books aren't love then I don't know what is. I have a lot of time to make up for—a lot of wounds to heal. I know now my grandparents lied to me. They led me to believe she didn't care. Perhaps they thought they were doing the right thing. I doubt we'll ever know, for they're dead now. The thing is, I've been given the chance to put things right with my mother. I spent the day with her and I think we made a start. Then I stayed at a friend's flat while I did some serious thinking. I knew I was in danger of losing what I wanted most—you. So I came home to tell you I loved you.'

Claudia moistened her lips. 'And found me gone.' The deception brought colour to her cheeks. 'I'm sorry about that, but I'm so happy for you and Nancy. When you love someone it's never too late. Will you be seeing her again?'

'We still have a lot to talk about. I said we'd invite them to the wedding, and she sent you her love,' Tyler admitted gruffly.

'I'd like that, and perhaps Oscar can give me away,' Claudia murmured, feeling as if her heart was so full that it might explode.

Tyler raised his head. 'It will cause quite a surprise. Equal to the one Natalie will get when we get home and tell her we're going to be married.'

Claudia's eyes danced. 'I think there are going to be a lot of surprises all round,' she said with a laugh, imagining his expression when Natalie turned up here in the morning.

Tyler half laughed, half frowned. 'What's so funny?'

She smiled. 'Nothing. Nothing at all.'

With a sigh he rolled on to his back, reversing their positions so that her head lay on his shoulder. 'Crazy woman,' he pronounced, and silently Claudia agreed that she was. Crazy in love with him, and she wouldn't have had it any other way.